W9-AUT-277

"I hope you're not making a mistake."

Matt made his comment from the doorway.

"Mistake? What mistake?" Jacqueline asked.

Impatiently he waved at the purchases she was carrying in. "It looks as if you're settling in. I'd save my money if I were you. You may not make it, you know."

Jacqueline's heart sank. "In case you haven't noticed," she said bitterly, "my intention is to stay and settle in, whether you like it or not!"

"I have noticed," Matt said coldly. "That's precisely why I'm making it very clear that I haven't yet decided whether you are staying. It would be wise to consider that before buying anything more."

Jacqueline seethed. How could a man be so unfair? It would be a pleasure to see his embarrassment when she proved him wrong!

WELCOME
TO THE WONDERFUL WORLD
OF *Harlequin Romances*

Interesting, informative and entertaining,
each Harlequin Romance portrays an appealing
and original love story. With a varied array
of settings, we may lure you on an African safari,
to a quaint Welsh village, or an exotic Riviera
location—anywhere and everywhere that adventurous
men and women fall in love.

As publishers of Harlequin Romances, we're
extremely proud of our books. Since 1949,
Harlequin Enterprises has built its publishing
reputation on the solid base of quality and
originality. Our stories are the most popular
paperback romances sold in North America; every
month, six new titles are released and sold at
nearly every book-selling store in Canada and the
United States.

A free catalogue listing all Harlequin Romances
can be yours by writing to the

HARLEQUIN READER SERVICE,
(In the U.S.) M.P.O. Box 707, Niagara Falls, N.Y. 14302
(In Canada) Stratford, Ontario, Canada N5A 6W2

We sincerely hope you enjoy reading
this Harlequin Romance.

Yours truly,

THE PUBLISHERS
Harlequin Romances

Sweet
Not Always

by

KAREN VAN DER ZEE

Harlequin Books

TORONTO·LONDON·NEW YORK·AMSTERDAM
SYDNEY·HAMBURG·PARIS·STOCKHOLM

Original hardcover edition published in 1979
by Mills & Boon Limited

ISBN 0-373-02334-0

Harlequin edition published May 1980

Copyright ©1979 by Karen van der Zee.
Philippine copyright 1979. Australian copyright 1979.
All rights reserved. Except for use in any review, the reproduction or utilization of
this work in whole or in part in any form by any electronic, mechanical or other
means, now known or hereafter invented, including xerography, photocopying
and recording, or in any information storage or retrieval system, is forbidden
without the permission of the publisher. All the characters in this book have no
existence outside the imagination of the author and have no relation whatsoever
to anyone bearing the same name or names. They are not even distantly in-
spired by any individual known or unknown to the author, and all the incidents
are pure invention.

The Harlequin trademark, consisting of the word HARLEQUIN and the portrayal
of a Harlequin, is registered in the United States Patent Office and in the Canada
Trade Marks Office.

Printed in U.S.A.

CHAPTER ONE

FOR weeks now Jacqueline had felt like a tightly wound up clockwork toy, madly running around in circles, dazed and confused. She'd been caught up in a whirlwind of frantic activity—applying for a visa, scheduling vaccinations, shopping, packing, saying goodbye to friends. There hadn't been time to think. But now, as she sat on the plane on her way to West Africa with nothing more to do than eat, read and sleep, a vague uneasiness suddenly washed over her. She wanted to go back to Ghana, no doubt about that, but was she up to the challenge of her new job? Did she really know what she was getting herself into? Living in a strange country with your parents was quite different from being there on your own, working for a living. Jacqueline had signed a contract for two years, but she hadn't even met the man she was going to work for. She stared out the window, seeing nothing but lush green tropical forest below. They were flying along the coastline of West Africa, but she wasn't sure where exactly they were. Liberia? The Ivory Coast? The sun was low, drenching the world in a golden glow, and in a matter of minutes it would be dark.

The uneasiness didn't go away and Jacqueline wasn't able to shake off her disturbing thoughts. Had she been over-confident in accepting the position of Administrative Assistant offered to her by International Food Production Incorporated? Memories of her interview with Christopher Jenkins in New York floated through her mind. *'It's a thankless, frustrating job, Miss Donnelly. I want this to be perfectly clear.'* His words came back to her now on a wave of panic. Don't be ridiculous, she told herself. Of course you can do it! Confidence and a hard head and some experience are what you need, and you have what it takes!

But her appearance was no plus point and she was painfully aware of it. The familiar feelings of inadequacy took hold of her again. If only she looked her age, she thought helplessly. If only she looked a little more ... *capable, competent.* But even now, at the age of twenty-three, people still treated her like a schoolgirl. And she knew she looked it with her curly blonde hair, wide blue eyes and a height of barely five foot two.

There was nothing she could do about it, only hope that it wouldn't influence her new boss's evaluation of her as a professional person.

Jacqueline had asked Christopher Jenkins about her new boss, Matt Simmons, and he had looked at her with a frown that had slightly disturbed her.

'He's tough, Miss Donnelly, and hardworking and totally dedicated. He'll demand every ounce of your capabilities.'

Well, she was tough, too. And hardworking and dedicated. And Matt Simmons was quite welcome to every ounce of her capabilities!

Someone touched her arm and she looked up into the clear grey eyes of the woman sitting next to her. Mrs Turner was short and comfortably round, radiating warmth and friendliness. 'You look tired, honey,' she said with the worried look of a mother.

'I've a bit of a headache,' Jacqueline answered. 'I'll see if I can find some aspirin.' She squeezed past Mrs Turner and her grey-haired husband and went in search of a stewardess.

They had been in the air now for more than ten hours and the interior of the plane showed signs of total ruin, as did the passengers. They lay sprawled out in their seats with utter abandon, their faces masks of mute resignation. Someone had dropped a dinner tray and food was everywhere. A howling baby kicked a cup of milk out of his mother's hand and Jacqueline barely escaped the splash. The child, the mother and the seat were dripping with the white liquid.

A stewardess handed her some aspirin and having swallowed them with some water, Jacqueline struggled back to her seat. Sitting down again, she glanced at Mr and Mrs Turner, wondering what they were thinking.

Mr Turner's warm brown eyes smiled at her. 'Just a little while longer,' he said. His face, tanned and weather-beaten, was all smiles and wrinkles and full of good humour. He was a Minnesota farmer and he and his wife were making the trip to see their first grandchild, a little girl, born in Accra. It had taken all their courage to decide to come to Africa and once they had found out that Jacqueline had lived in Ghana as a schoolgirl, they hadn't stopped asking her questions. What about the people? The food? The climate? And what about Jacqueline herself? Had she ever been bitten by a snake? Had she ever had malaria? How had she ended up in Ghana in the first place? Was her father a missionary?

'No, no,' she'd said, laughing. 'My father worked for the Agency for International Development.' She had told them a lot about herself and her family. That they had also lived in Switzerland and Turkey, and that she had always wanted to go overseas again after she finished college.

'Tell me about your job,' Mr Turner said. 'What will you be doing in a place like Accra?'

'I'm going to work for International Food Production,' she said. 'It's a private agency trying to help developing countries increase their food production.'

Being a farmer, Mr Turner was immediately interested, and had a hundred other questions Jacqueline tried to answer as best she could. After a while they fell silent and Jacqueline stared out the window. A swift darkness had settled on the country and she was sorry she couldn't see anything but a few lights here and there. She sighed. She couldn't wait to get out of the hot, stuffy plane with its stale smells of food, souring milk, cigarette smoke and warm plastic. She couldn't wait to walk into the Kotoka Airport building and be back in Ghana.

It seemed a long time before the plane finally began its descent. The passengers came back to life, dragging themselves out of their stupor. Frantic activity ensued. Seatbelts were fastened, various articles gathered and stuffed into bags and briefcases. Children wailed in unison as their parents hauled them out of the aisle and strapped them in their seats.

Excited and impatient, Jacqueline peered out the window, seeing Accra, ablaze with lights like a cluster of stars. Mrs Turner leaned over to look. Then she smiled and shook her head.

'A real city, it looks like. I feel so dumb. I think of Africa and all I can picture are mud huts, half-naked native girls and elephants.'

Jacqueline laughed. 'There are lots of mud huts, but you're not likely to run into any elephants in Ghana unless you go to the zoo.'

Mr Turner grinned. 'What about the half-naked girls?'

'I hate to disappoint you, but you'll find the people in Ghana very well dressed.'

'You're spoiling all my fun,' he said with a grimace.

The plane had landed and it was bedlam in the aisle as everybody tried to wrestle out of their seats at the same time. Mr and Mrs Turner squeezed in line and Jacqueline sat back in her chair, waiting until the situation had eased up. When she finally emerged from the plane, the hot, humid air hit her in the face. She grimaced. A steam-bath was not what she needed right now. As she stood in line for Customs, her body sticky with perspiration, her feet aching in her shoes, she wondered how she would recognise Matt Simmons. What had Christopher Jenkins said? Thirty-three, very tall, brown hair, brown eyes. Millions of men fit that description, although there wouldn't be that many of them in a place like Accra. But when she finally dragged her suitcases into the main lobby, she saw no one who even vaguely resembled the man she was looking for.

No one.

She had been one of the last passengers to come off the plane and most of the people had already left. There was no sign of Mr and Mrs Turner. Looking around once more, she knew she was alone and there was no one to meet her.

Now what? Frantically she searched through her mind for a course of action. It was after nine, too late to telephone. Nobody would be in the office at this hour. She had no idea where Matt Simmons lived, or where the office was located for that matter. I'm stuck, she thought with a mingling of anger and unease.

Several teenage boys stood crowding around her, fighting over who was going to carry which piece of luggage. Impatiently she turned. 'Two only,' she told them. 'The rest of you go.'

For a moment she looked around undecidedly and then she saw the Information desk. She'd try it for what it was worth. The girl in the booth was asleep with her head on her arms. When Jacqueline spoke to her she lifted her head and looked annoyed. She wore a straight-haired wig and her eyes were heavily made up.

'Yes?' she said unwillingly.

'I'd like to know if there's a message for me. My name is Jacqueline Donnelly.'

'What message?'

Jacqueline sighed. 'I've just come from New York, but there's no one here to meet me. I hoped someone might have left a message for me.'

The girl yawned. 'No, there's no message.'

Irritated, Jacqueline moved away. Why hadn't the girl said so in the first place?

She took a taxi to the Continental Hotel. It was the best hotel in town and she took it because she remembered it was close to the airport. She was tired and aggravated and she didn't care about the cost. If they couldn't bother to arrange for someone to pick her up, they'd better be prepared to pay the bill.

When she called the office the next morning, the only response was a disconcerting silence. She dialled again. Nothing. The office telephone was out of order. Disconnected. Something.

'Welcome to Ghana!' she said aloud to herself, slamming down the phone. Dejected, she sank down on the bed. Some reception this was! If Matt Simmons was so desperately in need of help, then where was he now? She looked through her papers, but the only other information she had was the post office box number, and that was of no use. Somehow she had to find the street address. A search through the telephone directory had no results. The operator had never heard of IFP. Now what? She bit her lower lip, suppressing a sense of rising fear. Was this a bad omen?

It took her more than an hour and several phone calls back and forth between the American Embassy and the Agency for International Development before someone thought it safe enough to give her IFP's street address. Who did they think she was? A spy from Russia?

She submitted herself to the mercies of another taxi driver, a mild-looking old man who drove like a maniac. The car was a classic. It shook and it rattled and it squeaked. The stuffing was coming out of the cushions and the side window wouldn't open.

The streets were teeming with life and Jacqueline took it all in with eager eyes. People were everywhere, standing or sitting on street corners, seemingly oblivious to the scorching sun and the deafening noise of the traffic. Women wrapped in colourful cloths walked by the road, carrying babies on their backs and shallow pans of oranges on their heads. There were rickety tables stacked high with loaves of bread, vegetable stands with baskets full of bananas and yams and coconuts. The sun glittered on the glass and metal of buses and passenger lorries swaying and shuddering down the road, emitting noxious fumes.

The driver raced down the ring road at death-defying speed, then slowed down as he turned into a smaller road. They jolted and bumped down narrow streets full of potholes, the driver honking at goats and children and nearly killing an absentminded chicken.

The two-storied building with its large blue sign wasn't difficult to find and Jacqueline sighed with relief as she climbed out of the car. The driver helped her carry her suitcases into the drab-looking reception room and accepted her money with a toothless grin.

A young girl behind a typewriter looked on curiously. She had no wig, but an intricate design of plaits decorated her head. Her make-up was immaculate and large gold hoops dangled from her ears. Jacqueline smiled at her.

'I would like to see Mr Simmons, please. My name is Jacqueline Donnelly.'

'Just a moment, please.' The girl's voice was soft and shy. She stood up, almost tripped and staggered away on her platform shoes. She was dressed in Western style, her skirt hem halfway down her calves. A moment later she came back and led Jacqueline down a dingy corridor into an air-conditioned office.

Matt Simmons was sitting behind a desk, writing, and Jacqueline watched him for a moment while he hastily signed some papers. Thick brown hair, curling around his ears, white, short-sleeved shirt, no tie. Then he raised his head and stood up, extending his hand. He was tall, very tall, towering over her meagre five foot two. His face was designed somewhat haphazardly, his nose crooked and too big, his eyebrows irregular. With his deep tan he looked as if he belonged on a tractor in the cornfields, rather than on a chair behind a desk. His hand was hard and strong as he grasped hers and Jacqueline wondered if a handshake really did characterise a man's personality. *'He's tough, Miss Donnelly, and hardworking and totally dedicated.'* The words echoed in her mind. Matt Simmons looked tough, no doubt about that.

She introduced herself, but there was no recognition in his dark eyes when she mentioned her name. The vague uneasiness she had felt all along suddenly grew alarmingly.

He held out a chair for her. 'Sit down, please.' He seated himself behind his desk and looked at her politely, impersonally.

'What can I do for you, Miss Donnelly?'

Jacqueline's mouth opened, then closed. *He didn't know! He didn't know who she was!*

'Mr Simmons, you ... you weren't expecting me?'

He frowned and looked down at his desk calendar. 'No, I'm sorry. I didn't realise we had an appointment.'

An appointment? Something was very wrong. She had

come halfway across the world to take this job and he did not even know she was coming.... She'd expected a warm welcome, friendly at least. Her apprehension grew into fear and she could feel it settling like a rock in her stomach. She swallowed.

'Mr Simmons, the head office in New York hired me three weeks ago. I'm your new Administrative Assistant.'

A sudden cold silence followed her words and she looked at Matt Simmons uneasily. Surprise, disbelief and anger chased each other across his face. His jaw muscles tightened and his eyes shot fire.

'Oh, no, you're not! There must be some mistake!' His voice exploded in the silence and she felt as if he had slapped her in the face. What did he mean? What was this all about? She stared into his stormy face, not comprehending. She took a deep breath.

'What do you mean—a mistake? You need an Administrative Assistant. They hired me. Here I am.'

His eyes were hard and forbidding as he looked at her. 'I have no idea what kind of a joke this is. I did not receive any information to the effect that they had found someone to fill the position. No letter, no telegram. Had I known, I certainly wouldn't have agreed to let you come. I very specifically requested a man for this job!' He leaned forward, looking her in the eyes, hard and unrelenting. 'This is nothing personal, Miss Donnelly, but I simply don't want you for this position!'

Shock silenced her and his words took a moment to settle. Then anger flooded through her and she could feel her face grow hot. 'May I remind you, Mr Simmons, that we're living in the seventies and that your attitude is extremely chauvinistic!'

He was not impressed. 'And may I remind *you* that this is not the United States of America, but Africa, and

that I have to deal with the realities of place and circumstances!'

'Which are?'

'I couldn't begin to tell you.' He groaned, raking impatient fingers through his unruly hair. 'My God, they
should have known better!'

Jacqueline was speechless with anger. *Who* should
know better? *He* was the one who should study the facts
before jumping to conclusions! Jacqueline was well
aware of the 'realities of place and circumstances.' She
knew it wasn't easy to get things accomplished in a place
where telephones didn't always work and car parts
weren't available when you needed them. Administrative
systems worked differently from at home and much more
slowly. It was a matter of survival to cultivate a patient
disposition and not get frustrated. Jacqueline also knew
that patience wasn't one of her stronger qualities. And
it was being severely tested this very minute.

She resented Matt Simmons's know-it-all attitude and
she desperately searched her mind for something to say.
Something crushing and damning. There was nothing.
Her mind was a blank.

For a long moment neither one of them said a word.
Then Matt Simmons suddenly raised his long frame out
of the chair and opened the door.

'Patience!'

Jacqueline heard fast footsteps clonking down the corridor and the girl with the plaited hair appeared in the
doorway.

'Yes, sir?'

'Bring me some coffee, please.' He turned to Jacqueline.
'Would you like some?'

'I'd rather have a drink,' she said drily, and saw a
shadow of a smile move around his lips.

'Sorry, no alcohol on the premises.'

'I'll settle for coffee, then. Strong, please.' She needed all the help she could get.

He sat down again and looked at her. He was not a handsome man, but his face was strong and square-jawed and very masculine. Oh yes, she thought bitterly, all man he is, pounding little old me down into the ground.

'So, what am I going to do with you now?'

His tone of voice infuriated her. Who did he think he was talking to? Some obstinate teenager?

'I suggest, Mr Simmons, that you forget that I'm a female and let me get on with the job.' She tried to sound calm and businesslike.

He raised one eyebrow and a sardonic smile flew across his face. 'It'll be rather difficult to forget you're a female. It's noticeable at a glance.'

Jacqueline looked at him coldly. 'Then I suggest you learn to live with the terrible truth. I'm here now and I have every intention of staying!'

'So I see.'

There was a knock on the door and the coffee was brought in.

'I'm sorry, but there's no sugar,' Matt said, handing her a cup from the tray. 'There's been a shortage for some time now.'

Jacqueline met his eyes. Was he expecting her to break down crying or jump up and down with indignation because she couldn't have sugar in her coffee? Well, he was in for a few surprises.

'Somehow I'll manage to suffer through it.'

He studied her with mockery in his eyes. 'In any case, it will help you keep your weight down. You must be all the way up to a hundred pounds.'

She didn't weigh much more than that and she knew she was short and thin and looked too young for her age, but that had nothing to do with her qualifications for the job. She just glared at him, not answering.

'Well,' he said, pulling his face straight, 'when did you arrive?'

'Last night.' She took a sip of the coffee, but it was too hot and she put the cup back on the desk.

'I'm sorry there was no one there to meet you.' It sounded as if he meant it. He shook his head. 'All this came as quite a surprise. I wonder what happened. Surely they must have sent me a telegram with the particulars of your arrival.'

Jacqueline shrugged. 'It's probably sitting at the P & T and someone neglected to deliver it.' It wouldn't be the first time. She'd seen it happen before.

He looked at her sharply. Then he grabbed the telephone on his desk, but slammed it down immediately. 'Damn thing is broken. Garbage truck drove under the wire and tore it down. It'll take weeks before they fix it.' He got up once more, opened the door and called for Patience again.

'I want Samson to go to the External P & T as soon as he comes back from the bank and see if there's a telegram from New York floating around on somebody's desk.'

'I'll tell him, sir.'

The girl disappeared and Matt closed the door.

'Well,' he said, sitting down again, 'what did you do when you found nobody waiting for you last night?'

'I found a taxi, went to the Continental Hotel, had a shower and went to bed.'

'And this morning?'

'I got up. Had breakfast. Traced you down.' She looked at him defiantly. What had he expected?

'Did you have the address?'

'Only the P.O. box and the phone number.'

'And the phone wasn't working.'

'Correct.'

They stared at each other for a moment, sizing each other up.

'So, how did you find the place?'

'I broke down and cried and my fairy godmother appeared and pointed the way.'

'You don't have to be sarcastic, Miss Donnelly.'

Her temper flared. All her anger and frustration came bubbling up and she couldn't stop herself.

'No, I should jump up and down for joy! I come halfway around the world to take a job—a job, mind you, that I've been looking forward to. I was told you were desperate for someone to help you out. And see what I get! A wonderful reception! A warm welcome! It is conveyed to me, in no uncertain terms, that since I am a female I'm no good for the job. I'm obviously considered incapable. It seems to surprise you that I can do as much as track you down without an address!'

'Calm down! Calm down! Let's talk this over rationally.'

She clenched her teeth and glared at him.

'Okay,' he said. 'Do you have a résumé with you?'

'No. Mr Jenkins told me they'd send it to you with the evaluation from the interview and my references.' She shrugged. 'I imagine that didn't arrive here, either.'

'No. The devil may know where that disappeared to.' He sighed. 'It will show up sooner or later. It usually does.' He drank the last of his coffee and pushed the cup away from him. 'I assume you have a degree?'

'Business Administration.'

His face registered no reaction. 'What did you do before you came over here?'

'I just graduated.' Which was part of the truth. She had also worked as the assistant manager of an old people's home and for several summers she had worked with Mexican migrant workers in California. She had taken the opportunities because they were valuable experience, although they had postponed her graduation for more than a year. Let him ask, she thought furiously. Let him think I'm just an incompetent female!

His reaction did not surprise her.

'You just graduated? They sent me a girl fresh out of school?' He groaned in utter despair. 'My God, they should have known better,' he said for the second time.

Jacqueline boiled inside. Stay calm, she told herself.

'They should have known *what* better, Mr Simmons?'

His face was hard, his eyes cold. 'That a business degree is nice, but experience abroad is more essential. Sitting in their comfortable offices in New York, they keep forgetting that working in this part of the world is a different story altogether. It takes different qualifications!'

'I see.'

He raised one mocking eyebrow. 'You do?'

Oh, yes, she did! One look at her and he had made up his mind. He didn't want any part of this dumb blonde, fresh out of college. It was a prescription for disaster. Nothing but incompetence, irritation and trouble. Oh, yes, she knew exactly what he was thinking!

'Listen, Miss Donnelly, I have no time to train someone for half a year, only to find out that she can't stick it out in this place. Have you had a good look around you? Have you heard of culture shock?'

'I believe so,' she said, keeping her face expressionless.

'This is not an ordinary job in an ordinary situation. There's nothing in any of your textbooks that could have taught you what you need to know. Time is the only teacher in this case. And time, Miss Donnelly, is what I don't have!'

'And Mr Jenkins in New York wasn't aware of this situation?'

His eyes narrowed in new anger. 'He damn well should have been! I've been quite explicit as to what type of person I need!' With an impatient move he shoved his chair back and got up. Hands in his pockets, he turned to the window and looked outside. Jacqueline stared at his back, broad and strong under the white shirt. His thick curly hair reached to his collar and could do with a cut. He was tall all right. At least six foot two, maybe more.

After a few silent minutes he sat down again, outwardly calm and composed. He folded his arms, tilted back his chair and gazed at her intently.

'Tell me, Miss Donnelly. Why the hell did they hire you?'

Jacqueline got up from her chair and grabbed the side of the desk. Her legs were trembling and the blood was pounding in her head. Of course, she could tell him now that she knew this country, and what was more, that she liked it. She could tell him that she had done a few other things besides going to college. But he wasn't asking, was he? No. And she would tell him exactly what he wanted to hear. Jacqueline smiled as sweetly as she could manage under the circumstances.

'They hired me, Mr Simmons, because I slept with the President!'

She turned and walked out of the room, closing the door carefully behind her.

CHAPTER TWO

SHE found the washroom and spent the next ten minutes trying to calm down. Her face in the mirror looked pinched and drawn. No wonder, after a long plane trip and a bad reception. This morning she'd put her long blonde hair on top of her head to stay cool, but some curly strands were falling down her face and neck. She combed it all out and pinned it back up. She washed her face, already damp with perspiration. It was one of the things she'd have to live with again, the continuous feeling of stickiness and heat. March was the worst month and the humidity made the heat almost unbearable.

But still she liked this place. For years she had wanted to come back to this country where she had spent three years as a schoolgirl. It wasn't any single thing that attracted her to Ghana, but a combination of many. Here she was free and safe in the streets, even alone. At any time of day or night. Ghanaians had a reputation for friendliness and hospitality and she loved the spirit of the women, their independence, their sense of humour. Despite the poverty and difficulties of life, there was never a lack of laughter and joy.

Jacqueline put her make-up and comb back in her shoulder bag and sighed. She'd been so anxious to be back, but now the shine of her enthusiasm had tarnished and she felt limp and deflated. She'd wanted to come back to Africa, make herself useful, do something that really mattered. And now this arrogant Simmons guy was trying to destroy it all for her. She threw one more glance in the mirror and straightened her shoulders. Well, she wasn't going to let him! She was staying, and she was going to do her job no matter what he thought of her.

The door opened and Patience came in. Her big eyes looked at Jacqueline shyly. 'Mr Simmons wants you,' she said, and Jacqueline almost laughed. Mr Simmons didn't want her, but he was going to have her whether he liked it or not!

She walked back into his office, head high, eyes cool. Ignoring his level gaze, she sat down. 'Mr Simmons, I'd like to know where I'll be staying so I can settle down and go to work. I was told you'd take care of the housing.'

His mouth curved faintly at the corners. 'That's what I wanted to talk to you about. We have a problem.'

'Tell me about it.'

'We have three hundred and fifty cedis in the budget to rent a house for the AA. Unfortunately that amount isn't nearly enough to get decent accommodation these days. There is an extreme shortage of houses and flats and in the last years rents have doubled, sometimes even tripled,' Jacqueline caught a glint of something in his eyes. Malice? Expectation? Was he challenging her?

'In other words, no house, no apartment. Correct?' She kept her voice calm, businesslike.

'Correct.'

If he expected her to go into hysterics, he'd have a long time to wait.

'What do you propose to do with me?'

He shrugged, face impassive. 'Ideally, I'd ship you back on the next flight.'

Jacqueline clenched her teeth. 'You can't fire me unless I fail to do my job adequately, and I plan to do it more than adequately,' she said with icy dignity.

'I'll give you a fair chance to show me your abilities, Miss Donnelly.' His face looked grim. 'As long as you're here and determined to stay, you might as well show me what you're worth. But I warn you, you'd better be good, because I have neither the time nor the inclination to babysit you. I need help and if you don't measure up, out you go, and the hell with Jenkins!'

Jacqueline ignored the tone of intimidation in his remark. If she were to deal with the man at all, she'd have to keep her cool. She took a deep breath.

'What about housing?'

For a moment he said nothing, then he sighed. 'If you could agree to the arrangement, you can have the guest flat in my house. It's a self-contained unit with its own entrance, bedroom, sitting room, and bathroom. But there's no kitchen. We'll have to share the one in the main part of the house.'

'Do I have a choice?'

'Not unless you want to find a place of your own and double the three-fifty out of your own pocket. Knowing the level of your salary, I doubt if you can afford it.'

She couldn't. But living in such close proximity to a man she disliked more by the minute was less than ideal, to say the least. For the time, though, it had to do.

'I'm not very particular,' she said. 'Let's see this place.'

The house was within walking distance from the office. It was an old colonial structure with large verandahs surrounded by an untamed, jungle-like garden in need of care. The large rambling rooms had creaking hardwood floors and squeaking ceiling fans. All the windows had burglar-proofing and mosquito screens.

'Your place is here,' Matt said, opening a door at the end of the main living-room/dining-room. She stepped into a small room with two glass doors leading on to a tiny verandah enclosed by blooming bougainvilleas. Opening other doors, she found the bedroom and the bathroom, both small but adequate.

'It's never been used,' he said, surveying the place with a frown. 'I've been using one of the bedrooms in the house for guests. It's more convenient.' He walked over to the windows and threw them wide open. The breeze somewhat freshened the warm, musty atmosphere. 'This place needs some work, that's clear,' he said. 'We'll have to get it cleaned and furnished. We'll start with some fresh paint. The whole house is in sorry shape, as you can see. That's why I got it cheap. You should have seen the kitchen before it was fixed up.' He turned and came a step closer, looking down on her with unconcealed challenge in his eyes.

'So, what do you think?'

'It's fine with me,' she said, meeting his eyes. 'All I need is a place of my own.'

'Well, for the time being, you'd better use the guest room. I'll have Kwesi start on this place right away. Come, I'll show you the kitchen and you can meet him.'

Heavy and muscular, Kwesi looked more like a boxer than a steward. He looked strangely out of place in the kitchen, stirring a pot of soup on the stove. Seeing them, his face came alive and he gave Jacqueline a broad, friendly smile when Matt introduced her.

'You are welcome,' he said, shaking her hand.

'*Medawasi.*'

Kwesi's grin grew wider, but Matt's eyes were full of mockery. 'Even learned some Twi, I see. Very commendable, but not entirely necessary. You do know the official language in this country is English?'

Ignoring his remark, Jacqueline looked in the pan on the stove. The kitchen was filled with the fragrance of the soup. She would have recognised it anywhere—palm-nut soup, brilliant red and spicy.

'Kwesi does the cleaning and the cooking,' said Matt, leading her out of the kitchen into the main room. 'I give him money for food and he decides what to feed me. He cooks mostly Ghana chop.' He cast her a brief, dark glance. 'It will take some getting used to, and if you like, you're welcome to teach him to fix some other things.'

Kwesi carried her suitcases to the guest room and they followed him in.

'Sorry, but the air-conditioner is broken,' Matt said, pointing at the hole in the wall. 'When it's fixed you can have it installed in your bedroom in the flat, but it will take a while. Everything here does. I'd give you mine, but that one is in the shop too, and God only knows when we'll get it back. Supposedly both the machines need new compressors, which were ordered nine months ago. The boat was due five months ago, but got re-routed someplace or some such thing—I don't remember the details.'

Frustration was all over his face and Jacqueline bit her lip to suppress a smile. Obviously he-man himself wasn't exactly immune to the trials and tribulations of life in Africa. Oh, how well she remembered! No sugar, no car tires, no spare parts of any sort. Ships that mysteriously disappeared or ended up in Shanghai or were stuck in the harbour for months. Not every Westerner could deal with that kind of frustration.

Matt looked at his watch, then raked impatient fingers through his hair. 'I've got to get back to the office—I have an appointment. I'll be back for lunch in an hour or so. See you then.' He strode out of the room, leaving Jacqueline to her own devices.

She sat down on the bed and stared at her suitcases. Should she unpack now, or wait until she got into her own place? Maybe she should have another look at the flat. As she entered the living-room, Kwesi came out of the kitchen.

'Would you like something to drink, madame? Coffee, or a mineral?'

'Something cold, please. Just water is fine.'

Kwesi frowned and looked troubled. 'We no boil the water, madame.'

'It doesn't matter, Kwesi. Accra water is safe enough, I'm sure.'

Kwesi grinned. 'Mr Simmons says so, but the missus, she boil the water fifteen minutes all the time.'

There had been no mention of Matt being married, and she looked questioningly at Kwesi. 'Mrs Simmons? Mr Simmons' wife?'

He shrugged his massive shoulders and smiled. 'Don't know. Maybe wife, maybe not,' he said casually.

Jacqueline frowned. If Matt had a wife, then what would she think of her living in the guest flat?

'Mrs Simmons isn't home?'

Kwesi shook his head as he opened the refrigerator and took out a bottle of water. 'She in the States, I think.'

Jacqueline didn't know what to make of it, but she did not want to ask Kwesi any more questions. She would find out from Matt. She had no intention of getting settled in the flat only to find later that the lady of the house, or whoever the 'missus' was, objected to her presence.

Kwesi handed her the glass of water with ice cubes in it and she carried it with her to the flat and looked around a little more carefully. Fresh paint and some good scrubbing would make a lot of difference. The mosquito screens were in bad shape and needed to be replaced. In the bathroom she flushed the toilet and it worked, much to her relief. A long trail of tiny ants wriggling across the tile caught her eye. She had forgotten about the ants. They were everywhere, even here in an unused, empty bathroom. One crumb of food left in the kitchen, on the table, on the floor, and in a matter of minutes a scouting ant had discovered it and called in the troops. They were the tiniest ants she'd ever seen anywhere, a harmless nuisance no amount of insecticide could get rid of. For three years her mother had fought a futile battle against them.

The wooden floor showed signs of serious neglect, but wax would help some, she hoped. She was delighted with the verandah. Bougainvilleas grew around it in profusion, showing an abundance of white and orange blossoms. She had the view of the back of the garden where untidy clumps of banana plants and a tall, majestic coconut palm stood together in an odd arrangement. To the right she could see the servants' quarters, partially hidden behind more bougainvillea. With some potted plants, chairs and a table, the verandah would be a lovely place to sit.

Matt appeared again an hour later and they sat down to a lunch of egg sandwiches and sliced pineapple.

'I have a couple of questions,' Jacqueline said.

'Fire away.' His dark eyes were on her and suddenly she felt uncertain, not knowing how to tactfully mention the subject of the 'missus.'

He noticed her hesitation. 'Getting cold feet?'

'No. I'm just wondering about living in the guest flat. Kwesi mentioned something about the "missus" and I wasn't aware you were married.' She flushed, feeling awkward. 'I mean, I don't know if your wife agrees with me living here, sharing the kitchen.'

He raised his eyebrows. 'Diane? She's not my wife,' he said flatly.

Embarrassment filled her. She didn't want him to think she was prying, but she had to know her position. 'I wasn't sure,' she said. 'I just don't want to be in the way. I mean, it's nice of you to offer me this place, but....'

'You won't be in the way,' he said shortly. 'Besides, she's not here now.'

'Oh.' Not knowing what else to say, she speared a piece of pineapple on her fork and brought it to her mouth. Looking up again, she found his eyes on her.

'And in case you're wondering, Diane left a couple of months ago because she can't stand this place, the heat, the hassles.'

Jacqueline said nothing.

His eyes were cold as he observed her. 'You may think you're pretty tough, but it takes a certain kind of person with a certain kind of stamina to survive in a place like this. This is no holiday resort, I can assure you.' He pushed back his chair and stood up. Jacqueline did the same.

'I didn't come here for a holiday!' she said, putting as much bite in her voice as she could.

'You'd better not!' He towered over her, looking down on her darkly. 'Besides the normal aggravations of daily life, you'll have to cope with a damn difficult job and, frankly, I have grave doubts whether you or any other little college girl can hack it!'

His intimidating behaviour infuriated her and she stared up into his eyes as hard as she could. No doubt he thought she was a typical dumb blonde, and her height didn't help. Never before had she wished more fervently that she was a tall brunette. At least she would look her age and wouldn't have to look up to this arrogant six-foot-plus male chauvinist.

'Your confidence is overwhelming,' she said, holding her eyes steady, cool. For a long moment their eyes locked. Then he smiled down at her and she saw how it softened the hard lines of his face. For a fraction of a moment it seemed as if she were looking at a different man.

'Of course,' he said slowly, 'there's always the odd chance that I'm mistaken.'

'Quite,' she said, smiling back at him.

She went back to the office with him to make her acquaintance with the other staff members. She'd already met Patience, the secretary-receptionist. Samson, the office messenger, was walking down the corridor as they entered the building. He was a young man, extremely thin, wearing very tight trousers and a tailored shirt. He assumed an air of importance as he shook hands with Jacqueline, but his somewhat sheepish grin spoiled the total effect. As he walked off, Jacqueline stole a glance at Matt and caught a glint of amusement in his eyes.

'Samson is a good kid, but he likes to impress people. He doesn't always carry it off with a lot of finesse.'

She smiled. 'So I noticed.'

. Matt led her into an office and introduced her to Mr Asanti, the office accountant. He was an older man, short and greying at the temples, wearing dark glasses that made him look like the African version of the jolly old professor of children's stories.

'Ofori and Lawani aren't here,' Matt told her, leading her out of Mr Asanti's office. 'They're assistant managers at the projects and they come to town only once or twice a month. You'll meet them later.' He gave a short rap on another door and pushed it open.

'Jacqueline, this is Steven Sowah, my right hand in agricultural matters—Steven, this is a surprise present from the head office, Jacqueline Donnelly, our new Administrative Assistant.'

The tall, broad-shouldered Ghanaian flashed her a brilliant smile. 'Pleased to meet you. I hope we can be friends, even after you've seen my expense reports.'

Matt groaned. 'His reports are a bookkeeper's nightmare. He knows all about goats, but he can't add a column of figures the same way twice.'

Steven grinned at Jacqueline. 'He doesn't like me, but I'm indispensable, so he's stuck with me.'

'So I've heard,' said Jacqueline, smiling. She remembered Christopher Jenkins singing Steven's praises. 'Your reputation is known far and wide.'

Matt raised his eyes heavenward in mock despair. 'He doesn't need that, Jacqueline! His head is too big already!' He manoeuvred her out of the room and they could hear Steven's loud laugh all the way down the corridor.

'Steven seems like a nice man.'

'First class, all the way around. Hard worker, too.'

'Christopher Jenkins told me about him.'

He cast her a glance full of irony. 'Well, I won't ask you what he told you about me.'

'Fairy tales. Nothing but fairy tales.'

One eyebrow shot up. 'Is that so? Now, I wonder why he did that.'

'The truth would have been too painful and too risky,' Jacqueline flashed back.

He thrust his hands into his pockets and leaned lazily against the wall, eyes narrowed. 'Risky?'

'Had they told the truth, they would never have found an AA to come here,' she said recklessly. 'Not even a dumb college girl like me.'

'Too bad,' he said sarcastically. 'Too bad you believed in fairy tales.'

Matt had an appointment and most of the afternoon he was out. Jacqueline talked at some length with Patience and Samson. In her new job she was in charge of the two of them and would have to co-ordinate their activities.

Her office was a small room off the main reception area where the clerical staff had their desks. The walls were painted a light green and the faded cotton curtains were a blue and brown African print. The linoleum was a dull grey and the whole room had a tired and dusty appearance. Jacqueline sighed. Then, looking through the window, she saw scarlet hibiscus and yellow-white frangipani. The bright colours cheered her up a bit and she positioned her desk so she had a view of the window. Samson dragged in an old wooden bookcase, a standing fan and an extra chair. This completed the decor. Looking at the drab surroundings, Jacqueline knew that she'd have to do something about the room's appearance or she would end up dusty and faded and tired too.

In the corner stood two large boxes filled to overflowing with paper. At closer inspection she recognised it as miscellaneous technical material on various aspects of agriculture. She tucked a damp strand of hair behind her ear and sighed again. There was a lot of work to be done in the office, no doubt about that. Obviously Patience had no idea of proper organisation and it would take a considerable amount of time to bring some sort of order into the office procedures. But she was determined, now more than ever, that she was going to do everything in her power to prove that she could do it. An uneasy thought stirred her mind. Was her job the real challenge? Or was it Matt?

That night they had dinner together and she was aware of Matt's amusement when she gave herself a generous helping of palm-nut soup, rice and fried plantain.

'Be careful,' he said. 'It's very hot. Kwesi uses red pepper with a very liberal hand.'

'I will, Mr Simmons.'

'There's no need to be so formal. Suppose you can manage to call me Matt?'

'I'll try, if you insist,' she said coolly.

'I insist, Jackie.'

'*Jacqueline!*' she said sharply. Her friends could call her Jackie, but not this arrogant stranger.

He reclined his head slightly, mocking her. 'Jacqueline it is.'

The food burned in her throat, but she was familiar with the sensation. She pretended not to notice that Matt watched her closely while she ate. As a girl she had enjoyed the spicy Ghanaian food. With her friend from the International School she had often eaten at the roadside chop bars. She had tasted everything from squid to snails, much to the horror of her mother, who feared that she would pick up some dreadful germ and die of dysentery. It had never given her even the slightest indigestion.

Matt was staring at her across the table as she finished her food and she smiled at him defiantly.

'It's good. I enjoyed that.'

He frowned. 'You may be sorry tomorrow. Weren't you overdoing it a little?'

'I've a stomach of cast iron, don't worry about me.'

'Pretty tough all the way around, aren't you?'

Jacqueline nodded. 'Who knows? Maybe even tough enough for Ghana.'

He could make fun of her all he wanted. One day he'd be sorry. She didn't like the feelings of animosity growing inside her. Fighting some sort of personal battle with her boss wasn't her idea of a good working relationship.

'Something wrong?' Matt asked, as if he had guessed her thoughts.

'I'm just tired,' she said irritably. 'I think I'll go to bed early.'

The next morning she woke up to the sounds of cackling chickens and clanking buckets. For one short, elusive moment she didn't know where she was. This seemed like a new world with strange sounds and sensations that somehow still carried a faint hint of familiarity. Even the light was different, hard and bright already so early in the morning. Heat and humidity were carried in on the breeze that blew through the open window and the overhead fan stirred the air in a feeble attempt at coolness.

Africa. Ghana. It all came back to her then on a wave of joy and excitement. For a few moments she lay very still in the sun-drenched room, watching the curtains billow in the ocean breeze, listening to the sounds coming from outside—a rooster's crow, the crying of a child, the voice of a woman calling out in a language she didn't understand.

Then she threw off the sheet, leaped out of bed and looked outside. A small girl was filling a bucket under a tap outside the servants' quarters. In the shade of a huge mango tree a woman sat on her haunches stirring a pot simmering on a small charcoal burner. A colourful cloth covered her from chest to ankles, leaving her shoulders bare. A naked baby crawled in the red dirt, playing with a hard, green mango.

Kwesi's family? Probably. The baby plopped over on his fat little bottom and started wailing. The mother abandoned her stew and put the baby on her lap. She took out her breast and the baby grabbed it with eager little hands and began to drink. Jacqueline watched the little scene for a moment and then turned away from the window. It was wonderful to be back in Africa and she felt light and happy, ready for the day.

She showered and dressed in a light cotton dress and leather sandals. It would be too warm to let her hair down, so she pinned it up again. Before coming to the tropics she had considered cutting it off, but she hadn't had the courage to do it. It would take years to grow back.

She found Kwesi in the kitchen preparing breakfast.

'Good morning, Kwesi.'

'Good morning, madame.'

'Is that your family I saw outside, Kwesi? The little girl and the baby?'

'Yes.' His smile was wide and proud. 'I have another son, but he lives in my home village with my wife's mother.'

'Where's your village?'

'Mankessim. It's on the road to Cape Coast.'

Jacqueline chatted with him for a while, then left him so he could finish cooking breakfast. The verandah doors were open and she stepped outside, taking in all the colour and brightness of the morning. Was there no gardener? she wondered, surveying the masses of greenery and bushes grown wild. Some cutting and trimming certainly seemed in order.

Some swift movement caught her eyes and she saw two lizards chasing each other on the wall of the house, racing down and across the verandah and then leaping off into the bushes.

'Quite a jungle, isn't it?' It was Matt's voice behind her. He looked clean and fresh in grey slacks and a white shirt.

'A bit. I like a lot of greenery, though.'

'No shortage of that here. We have a gardener who comes twice a week to keep things under reasonable control, but he's been gone for a month. He had to go back to his village because his grandfather was sick.' He shrugged. 'Can't tell when he'll be back.'

'There are a lot of banana plants here,' Jacqueline commented, looking at the untidy bushes huddled in the corner of the garden.

'Yes. But don't try to eat those over there.' He pointed

at some plants by the side of the drive. 'They're not bananas.'

The plants looked identical, but if they were not bananas then there was only one other thing they could be.

'Plantain,' she said. It was a statement, not a question, and he looked at her with a flicker of surprise in his eyes.

'How do you know that?'

She shrugged lightly. 'I know a lot of things.'

'Oh, you do?' The derision in his voice was unmistakable.

She raised her eyebrows and looked at him wide-eyed. 'Shouldn't I? I just graduated from college!' With that she left him on the verandah and went inside to help Kwesi.

Matt was cool and polite at breakfast and as soon as they were finished they left for the office. It was barely seven.

'We'd better get started early. I'm swamped with work and we have to get your job outlined for you and see how we can organise your work.'

When she had been in his office the day before she had not noticed the surroundings. The room was as drab as her own, with dull floor tiles and faded green-blue tie-dye curtains. The laborious gasping and groaning of an air-conditioner in need of cardiac repair served as appropriate background music.

He was businesslike and impersonal as he talked to her about her work, showing her reports and charts and files, explaining the inner workings of the office.

'You'll be in charge of the clerical staff—Patience and Samson, as I said yesterday. You'll do the payroll, bookkeeping and financial reports. You'll have to devise some sort of system for them.'

'Yes, I can see that,' Jacqueline answered, looking at

the stack of papers on his desk.

He looked up, frowning. 'I just haven't had time. Besides, I hate administration. The files—you'll have to do something about the files, too.'

Jacqueline had already had a look the day before. The files were a mess beyond description. File folders were simply numbered and the contents written next to the number. *Bank of Ghana*, *Maize Production*, *Farm Machinery* were all cosily grouped together in the drawers.

'Patience told me she deals with the files,' Jacqueline said. 'I'll have her help me sort them out.'

'She knows where everything is, strange as it may seem. She can find every scrap of paper ever filed.' He grimaced. 'Of course, no one else can.'

'What about the cars? I was told it's a major effort to keep them on the road.'

'Yes. And I'm only too glad to hand that headache over to you, too. There's a shortage of parts, they're not fixed properly and they're forever breaking down in the most inconvenient places.'

They dealt with everything from banking to goat farming to car repairs, and by lunch time Jacqueline was dead tired. She was stuffed full of information she couldn't possibly digest all at once.

At home, Kwesi had prepared fish sandwiches and fruit salad and she sat at the table facing Matt, too tired even to chew. The hot air enveloped her like a Turkish steam bath and she could feel the perspiration trickling down her back. Her hair was coming loose on the side and she pulled it behind her ear, feeling the dampness of it and the clamminess of her skin.

'I'll be busy this afternoon,' said Matt, looking at her closely. 'I have a meeting with AID—pardon me, the Agency for International Development. So why don't you stay home and catch up on some sleep? By the looks of you, you're suffering from an acute case of jet lag.'

She gave him a dull smile. 'Wonderful idea. I think I'll do just that.' At the door she turned and faced him. 'Matt?'

'Yes?'

'What did you say AID stands for?' Her face was innocent, but the hint of sarcasm in her voice apparently hadn't escaped him. He stared at her for a long moment, face unreadable.

'I think you heard me, college girl.'

On Thursday morning Matt handed her a pile of documents.

'Well, let's see what you can do with this.'

Jacqueline looked at the papers in her hand. Shipping documents of some sort, she guessed. 'What is this?' she asked.

'It's equipment for the rice project. It's at the airport, ready for pick up.'

'Okay, I'll get it.'

He looked at her, frowning. 'It's not as easy as it sounds. You'd better leave as soon as possible, or you won't make it back before lunch. The red tape is indescribable, and if they hassle you about import duty, don't give an inch. This stuff is duty free, no matter what they tell you. Raise hell if you have to.' He looked at her doubtfully. 'You think you can do it?'

She was well aware of what he was thinking. Those men out there would take one look at this dumb blonde and walk right over her. Well, here was her first chance to prove herself.

'I don't know why not,' she answered coolly.

He shrugged. 'Just one thing. Money works wonders in a place like this, but under no circumstances do we pay dash. I want that to be perfectly clear!'

She straightened her shoulders and glared at him. Bribery was common enough and a very practical tool indeed, but it wasn't one she happened to believe in.

'Don't worry about my moral values! They were checked out carefully in New York.'

'Good,' he said flatly.

Getting the equipment out of the airport cargo building was a good introductory experience in being patient and cool. Easy it was not. She was sent from one desk to the next, from one building to another and back again, filling out forms, writing signatures, fifteen in all, waiting, staring at dirty walls and dusty files piled high in the corners. A clerk was sleeping on his typewriter. Jacqueline wished she could do the same. The heat and the still air drained her of energy.

If all of this wouldn't have been such an utter waste of time, she wouldn't have felt so frustrated. But there was nothing she could do about it, and she certainly wasn't going to mention it to Matt. There was no doubt in her mind that he was testing her, and that he would be doing that for a while to come.

It took more than two hours before she finally arrived at the Customs desk. The officer smiled at her and helped her open the cartons.

'Industrial equipment?'

'Yes, sir.'

He studied the papers. 'For a rice mill, I see.' He stamped the papers and handed her the boxes.

Jacqueline returned to the office feeling rather jubilant about her victory and wondering what Matt's reaction would be. She knocked and entered his office, putting the boxes on his desk.

'It's all here. No damage as far as I can see.'

Matt looked from Jacqueline to the boxes and back

again. 'You got them?' He seemed surprised.

'Of course.' So he had been testing her. He hadn't really thought she could manage. Well, she had, and she was going to continue doing so.

He frowned, raking his fingers through his hair. 'They gave you no trouble?'

'Nothing I couldn't handle,' she said quietly. 'Why?'

He shrugged, taking the boxes and opening them. 'They have a reputation.'

No doubt he expected her to complain like everybody did—about the long waiting, the endless number of signatures, the shuttling back and forth from desk to desk. She said nothing. She wasn't going to give him the satisfaction.

'Is there anything else?' she asked instead.

He was examining the contents of the boxes and he looked up, shaking his head. 'No, but it's time for lunch. Are you ready?'

After lunch Jacqueline went out again, searching round town for filing cabinets and some other office supplies. The town had not changed much and Jacqueline had no trouble finding her way around. The streets were crowded with people and honking vehicles. Taxi drivers shouted obscenities at pedestrians and vendors sat on the pavement with their wares spread out in front of them—cough mixtures and shoelaces and dog chains and talcum powder and underwear and native medicines. Walking carefully on the uneven pavement, trying not to step into the open gutters, Jacqueline went from shop to shop.

In the Kingsway Department Store she found herself suddenly face to face with Mr and Mrs Turner and their daughter-in-law. After enthusiastic greetings and introductions, they all went to the coffee shop and had a cool drink. Lisa was a pretty girl with short, glossy black hair and large luminous eyes framed by oversized glasses. Jacqueline was invited to dinner on Saturday night and she gratefully accepted. Making friends was not difficult in a place where so many people were foreigners, and Jacqueline looked forward to getting to know Lisa better. It would be nice to know some other people. Everyone she had known before had moved on to other places—it was the way the expatriate community lived. No one stayed more than a few years in any one place.

On Friday night Jacqueline moved into her flat, which still smelled of paint and wax. Kwesi and three of his friends had spent the last two days getting the place ready for her and a carpenter had come to put up new mosquito screens. The speed at which all this had happened was quite astonishing, even considering the number of people involved. It wasn't the best paint job she'd ever seen, but it would do. The off-white walls looked clean and fresh now and the wooden floor had a shine of sorts.

On Saturday morning she did some shopping for herself in the Makola market, the giant open market in the centre of town. As a schoolgirl she had spent hours there searching for special kinds of beads or lengths of cloth for a dress.

The sun blazed down on her head and she could feel the sweat drip between her breasts and down her back, soaking her dress. There wasn't a breath of air in the crowded market where people thronged in slowly moving masses between the stalls. Women with heavy loads on their heads elbowed their way through the narrow alleys. Jacqueline looked around with fascination, taking it all in with greedy eyes. Baskets, clay pots, beads and native medicines were spread out for inspection. Vegetables were neatly arranged in small piles—tomatoes, garden eggs, hot peppers, okra. The meat looked less than appetising—pink hogs' feet, dried fish and shrimp. The smell was overpowering and Jacqueline moved on, looking for the stalls where she could buy material for curtains.

It was difficult to make a choice from the large variety of brightly coloured African prints that lay piled high in the stalls or hung neatly over racks in six- or twelve-yard lengths. Sitting on low stools, the market mammies watched her with interest as they were suckling their infants or stirring boiling pots of soup. Trying out her rusty Twi, she was soon surrounded by more women and children and they joked and laughed with her until she had made her choice and bought the cloth she needed.

With a retinue of little girls carrying her purchases, she rounded up a taxi and went home.

Kwesi came out to help her unload her things and Matt stood in the doorway, looking at her with an angry twist around his mouth.

'I hope you're not making a mistake,' he commented.

'Mistake? What mistake?'

Impatiently he waved at the pots, the baskets, the material. 'It looks as if you're settling in. I'd save my money, if I were you. You may not make it, you know.'

Jacqueline's heart sank and she bit her lip. Every time she was in high spirits, he found a way to spoil her mood. She was hot and tired and irritation burned in her throat. 'In case you haven't noticed,' she said bitterly, 'my intention is to stay and settle in, whether you like it or not!'

'I have noticed,' he said coldly. 'That's precisely why I want to make it very clear to you that I have by no means decided yet that you are staying. It would be wise to take this into consideration on further shopping expeditions.' He turned on his heel and walked inside, leaving Jacqueline seething on the verandah. She was glad she was getting out of the house tonight. The dinner at the Turners' would be a welcome diversion.

Kwesi told her that lunch was ready, but all feeling of hunger had left her and she had no desire to sit across from Matt, making polite conversation.

'Kwesi?'

'Yes, madame?'

'Would you mind bringing me some fruit salad here? And a big glass of water? I don't want anything else.'

'Yes, madame.' He looked at her searchingly. 'Are you not feeling fine?'

Jacqueline smiled. 'I'm just tired, Kwesi, that's all. Makola Market is an exhausting experience for an Obruni.'

In her bedroom, she stripped off her clothes, took a shower and washed her hair. It felt good for a few glorious moments, but soon she'd be hot and sticky all over again. It would be nice if she could get an air-conditioner in her room. The fruit salad and the water were on the table when she came back into the sitting room and she ate and drank slowly, too tired to put much effort into it. She found a book and collapsed on her bed. The rest of the afternoon she spent in exhausted sleep.

She had no idea where the Turners lived and it had been agreed that Lisa's husband would come for her at half past seven. Jacqueline put on a long cotton dress in blues and greens and piled her hair high on her head. Little curls stubbornly escaped and framed her face and she tried to smooth them back without much success.

As she was putting on her high-heeled shoes there was a loud knock on the inside door. It was Matt, dressed in jeans and a T-shirt, looking at her sardonically, one eyebrow raised.

'There's a Mr John Turner waiting for you in the

living-room. You want me to bring him here?'

'No, thanks. I'm ready.' She made a mental note to tell people to come to her own front entrance.

Matt leaned casually against the doorpost, hands thrust in his pockets. His gaze travelled over her and there was a glint of admiration in his eyes.

'Quite a lady,' he commented.

She ignored his remark and picked up her handbag.

'Excuse me,' she said when he didn't move. 'I'd like to pass, please.'

He stepped aside. 'For a little girl it didn't take you long to start swinging.'

Anger crept up inside her and she clenched her teeth. Why couldn't he leave her alone? She moved past him, looking up into his face.

'That's the advantage of being a dumb blonde,' she said coolly. 'Never a dull moment.'

He threw back his head and laughed out loud.

John Turner was a handsome man, the type one saw in advertisements for male fashions—lots of white teeth and every hair in place. No wonder Matt thought she was a fast mover. What a catch this man would be! Jacqueline laughed inwardly at the thought. He wasn't her type—too smooth for her taste. She preferred a less polished look.

They went outside and John opened the car door for her, then came around the other side and got in behind the wheel.

'My parents told me all about you,' he said, smiling. 'It's nice to have someone to talk to on that flight. It's murder, isn't it?'

'No fun,' she acknowledged.

'We live in North Labone,' he said, manoeuvring the car around Danquah Circle. 'Do you know it?'

Jacqueline nodded. 'Yes. I used to live in Cantonements with my parents, right at the edge of North Labone.'

The Turners' house was large and beautiful and, to Jacqueline's relief, fully air-conditioned. The coolness was refreshing after the damp heat outside and it would make it so much more pleasant to eat a hot meal.

Lisa and John's parents greeted her warmly and she was guided to a chair and furnished with a frosty gin and tonic. Mr and Mrs Turner enthusiastically started telling her about their experiences of the last few days, but they couldn't decide who was telling what and who should speak first. Their words and phrases came tumbling out in odd mixtures. Lisa started laughing, and John shook his head.

'I think they've enjoyed themselves so far,' he said. 'How about you?'

Yes, what about her? No, she had not enjoyed herself, and no, she was not very enthusiastic about her new boss. And no, she certainly couldn't tell them about that. So she smiled.

'I'm glad to be back in Ghana,' she said. Which was the truth. 'There was a little mix-up about my arrival, but I'm settled in now and ready to throw myself into the job.'

'Don't kill yourself,' John said. 'Easy does it in this climate.'

A little later the steward announced that dinner was served and they all went into the dining-room and seated themselves. There was a cheese soufflé and chicken in wine sauce and apple pie for dessert.

'It looks delicious,' Jacqueline said to Lisa. 'You must have made a trip to Lomé lately.' She remembered her mother's shopping excursions across the border into Togo, where everything imaginable was imported from France, including drinking water.

Lisa laughed. 'How did you guess? I go once a month or so. It's worth the hassle. Would you like to come along some time?'

Jacqueline could imagine what Matt would say if she told him she needed the day off to go grocery shopping in Togo.

'I'd like to, but not for a while. I'm just starting my new job and to take a day off to go to the supermarket probably isn't what my boss has in mind for me at this point.'

'I forgot you're a working girl. Well, let me know if you need anything. I'll be glad to bring it back for you.'

Jacqueline had a wonderful evening, feeling carefree and happy, as if some dark shadow had slid away and she could breathe again and enjoy herself.

Later that night John took her home and as they approached the house Ali, the watchman, opened the gates and they crunched up the gravelled drive.

'Thanks for the ride, John. I had a wonderful evening.'

He smiled, showing large white teeth. 'You're welcome. You know where we live now, so come by any time. Make it during the day some time, then you can admire our beautiful bald daughter.'

'Poor kid!' Jacqueline laughed as she climbed out of the car. 'Nine months old and still no hair.' They said goodnight and John drove away.

As she turned the corner of the house, the front door to her flat flew open and Matt's long frame came into sight, silhouetted against the light coming from her sitting room.

A sudden hot anger flared through her. This was *her* flat! What did he think he was doing, standing there in *her* doorway!

CHAPTER THREE

HE said nothing as she walked up to him, just stood there watching her, waiting for her to open the conversation. Well, she'd have no problem doing that.

She glared at him furiously. 'May I ask you what you're doing in my apartment?'

He thrust his hands into his jeans pockets and looked down on her calmly. 'Oh,' he said lazily, 'just looking.'

'Just looking! What gives you the right to go snooping around in my place?'

'Snooping? Who said anything about snooping?'

'*I* did!' Swiftly she moved past him into the sitting room and he followed her, closing the door behind him. Noises from the bathroom startled her and she stood still in the middle of the room. Through the closed door the muffled voice of an excited sportscaster reached her ears and she looked at Matt, totally flustered.

'What's *that*?'

'A radio broadcasting the boxing match from the stadium.'

Jacqueline pointed at the bathroom. 'Who's in there?'

'Kwesi.'

She sighed. 'How about telling me what's going on here?'

'You haven't given me much of a chance, have you?'

Exasperated, she turned and as she opened the bathroom door the voice of the sportscaster blasted in her ears.

Water. Water everywhere. And in the middle stood Kwesi, barefoot and with his pants legs rolled up, fight-

45

ing the flood with a mop and bucket. The transistor radio stood on top of the toilet tank. It took a moment to absorb the scene. Then she quickly closed the door, blocking out the screaming and the shouting of the spectators. Matt was sitting in a chair watching her with sardonic eyes.

'Considering the circumstances, am I forgiven for intruding in your holy of holies?'

Jacqueline nodded numbly and sank into a chair. 'What happened?'

'One of the pipes broke. Ali discovered it when he made his rounds. The bathroom window was open and he heard the water coming out full blast. He knew you weren't home, so he came and told me. The rest you can guess.'

Jacqueline sighed. 'I suppose the bathroom will be out of commission for a while.'

'Depends on how fast you can get it fixed,' he said laconically. 'I'll give you the name of the plumber on Monday. I'm sure you'll be able to cope with this emergency adequately.'

'Thank you very much,' she said drily.

'It's all part of that glamorous job of yours,' he said, grinning.

'I'm quite aware of that.'

'Well, I'm not needed here any more, so I'll be off.' He rose and strode over to the connecting door.

'Oh, by the way,' he said, turning to face her, 'while you're dealing with the plumber, tell him to come to the office and fix that leaky tap. And you might as well follow up on the phone wire and the air-conditioners, too. I'll give you the details on Monday.'

Before she could think of a suitable reply he had closed the door behind him.

Wearily she kicked off her shoes and a wave of fatigue

washed over her. Too much had happened in the last few days to assimilate all at once—her lonely arrival, the less than warm reception, her disastrous relationship with Matt. All the work at the office suddenly seemed a hopeless task and she was overwhelmed by the sheer bulk of it. Her nights were hot and uncomfortable and she slept badly. In the mornings she awoke sticky and sweaty and still tired.

And now this. This stupid water pipe! Nothing worked in this place! The bathroom, the telephone, the air-conditioners! Here she was, less than a week in the country and it was all piling up on her—the aggravations, the irritations and a boss who was contributing to it. He was putting on the pressure, loading her up with work and wearing her out. Oh yes, she knew what his intentions were. He'd have her back on that plane in no time at all, because sooner or later she'd collapse under the strain.

Kwesi entered the sitting room carrying the mop and bucket and his transistor radio. He looked wet and dishevelled, but he was smiling.

'Is finish now. There was plenty water! Plenty, plenty!'

Jacqueline gave him a tired smile. 'Thank you so much, Kwesi. I'm sorry we had to call you in on your night off.'

He shrugged. 'I was listening to the boxing match and I just brought the radio with me while I was working.'

'Well, I'm glad you didn't have to miss it. Who won?'

'D. K. Poison. My favourite.'

Jacqueline smiled. 'Good for you.'

He made for the door, but she called him back. 'Kwesi, do you know a seamstress somewhere close by? I bought some material in the market to make curtains, but I need someone to sew them for me.'

He smiled proudly. 'My wife has a sewing machine.

She make dresses and everything. She can sew curtains for you. I tell her.'

'Wonderful! I'll come and talk to her tomorrow. Will she be home?'

He nodded. 'She go to church in the morning, but then she is home.'

'Okay, thank you, Kwesi.'

'Oh, I want to tell you. Mr Simmons, he close off the water, so you have to use the other bathroom.'

'Thank you, Kwesi. Goodnight.'

'Goodnight, madame.'

Depressed and miserable, Jacqueline went to bed.

The next morning she felt better. She made herself some tea and toast and took it to the verandah on a tray. It was very early, barely six o'clock, and Accra was very quiet and peaceful. Everyone seemed to be still asleep and from the surrounding houses no noises came. A chicken and her brood wandered through the garden, scratching the ground here and there, searching for food. The anxious chirping of the chicks filled the air for a while until they disappeared through the hedge in search of more nourishment elsewhere. A big black bird with a white chest sat on a electricity wire in majestic silence, surveying the world about him as if he were the king of creation.

Jacqueline drank her tea slowly, enjoying the early morning atmosphere. What should she do with this Sunday? Write letters? Read a book? Measure and cut the curtains? If she could find a vase or a jar she could bring in some of the bougainvillea branches and brighten up the room. She stretched out comfortably in her chair. It would be nice to have a peaceful day away from that hectic, disorganised office. And away from Matt, if she could avoid him in the house. Matt. It was hard not to think about him even when he wasn't around; it was hard to ignore him when he was. His very presence seemed to fill the room he was in. He radiated a kind of electricity that was impossible not to be aware of. She sighed and closed her eyes.

The world slowly awakened. A car carefully turned the corner without the usual honking. Lufthansa flew over. Jacqueline listened to the sound as it dissolved in a low rumble, then disappeared. A baby cried. Voices came from the servants' quarters. Someone laughed. She heard water running and the sounds of pots and pans. The day had begun.

Cutting and basting the curtains took longer than she had anticipated and it was afternoon before she was finished. From Kwesi's house came the rhythmic sounds of someone pounding *fufu* and Jacqueline walked over to the small cement building, the curtains draped over her arm. On the little verandah she found Evelyn, Kwesi's wife, with a huge wooden pestle in her hands pounding starchy balls of yam in a big mortar. Another woman sat on her haunches, moving the *fufu* balls around in the mortar with swift, expert movements, avoiding the pestle as it came down hard and fast. Both women were wrapped in colourful cloths covering them from chest to ankles. Seeing Jacqueline, they stopped their work and looked at her shyly.

'I wonder if you would mind sewing these curtains for me?' Jacqueline asked. 'I've already basted them.'

Evelyn nodded. 'Kwesi tell me. I can do it.' She took the material from Jacqueline. 'It is nice cloth. You get it in the market?'

'Yes, I bought it yesterday. When do you think you can do it?'

'Tomorrow. I think tomorrow.'

'Good! How much shall I pay you?'

They agreed on a price and Jacqueline walked back to her apartment while the women resumed their meal preparations.

The curtains were finished when promised and the whole flat took on a new appearance. It started looking like home.

There was more to cheer her up in the following weeks. She had the water pipe replaced, the telephone wire repaired and the air-conditioners reinstalled, all within ten days. Not even Jacqueline had hoped for such tremendous efficiency. She had accomplished it with cold calculation and sheer persistence. Constantly checking up on the progress of the repairs, she had made a very pleasant and polite nuisance of herself. It had taken a lot of concentration on her part since her temper flared so easily. She had smiled and joked and kept coming back every day, sometimes twice, until finally the men in charge had obliged her just to get rid of her.

'How did you manage to get all that done so fast?' Matt asked her, scrutinising her closely.

'Don't worry, I didn't pay any dashes.'

'What *did* you do? Seduce the foremen?'

If he wanted to be vulgar, so could she. She looked at him, innocent, wide-eyed.

'Is there any other way?'

The next month Jacqueline worked furiously organising her work, systematising the files. Working with Patience, she'd realised that she would have to do the initial sorting of material herself—not a job she relished doing since it took an enormous amount of time to sort through the stacks of dusty papers that she found in boxes and cabinets. Most of it wasn't used often, but it had to be kept as a source of information. At least, she thought with a sigh, she had learned a few things about maize storage, groundnut cultivation and chickenfeed.

Almost finished one night, she worked late, losing all track of time. She worked in a trance, like an automaton. It was the only way to get this awful job done.

Suddenly, in the silence of the quiet office, she heard the front door bang and Matt's long frame appeared in the doorway. He looked clean and fresh, his hair wet. Straight out of the shower, no doubt. She was suddenly aware of herself, sitting in the middle of the dusty stacks of papers, sticky and dirty. Her nose and throat were dry from the dust collected by the mounds of paper and set free by her sorting and rearranging.

Matt stared at her in amazement. 'I wondered where the hell you were,' he said. 'Don't you think you're overdoing it a bit? It's after seven.'

Resentment bubbled up inside her. 'You don't have to pay me overtime, so don't worry about it,' she answered coldly.

'Well, why don't you call it a day and come home and we'll have something to eat.'

'I'm not ready yet. You can tell Kwesi not to wait for me. I'll fix myself something when I come home.'

'It's Kwesi's day off.'

Jacqueline shrugged. 'Oh, I forgot.'

'There's no need for you to work like this!' His voice exploded with sudden, sharp irritation. 'You need your rest! First thing you should learn is that in this climate you can't work like you do at home! Your system won't take it!'

She clenched her hands in her lap. Why didn't he leave her alone? She could take care of herself. She did not need his constant interference.

'I'll take care of my system, thank you!'

His face hardened and a dangerous glow came into his eyes. 'If you think you're going to impress me by working like a maniac, you're sadly mistaken! Getting yourself overworked isn't the way to go about it!'

'Leave me alone! I'll do *my* job the way *I* see fit!'

There was a silence loaded with electricity. She did not avert her eyes. Matt's mouth was a hard, straight line.

'All right,' he said slowly, 'do as you please.' He stalked out of the office and she heard the front door slam, then the car started and he was gone.

I know what he was thinking, Jacqueline thought. *Why bother? The sooner she cracks up, the sooner I'm rid of her.*

It was very quiet around her. She looked down again at the papers in front of her, but her eyes burned and she realised she was hungry and thirsty. It was Kwesi's day off, Matt had said. Had he been waiting for her to come home and cook dinner? Tough luck, brother. He could do his own cooking.

Concentration had gone with the interruption of his coming and she wasn't able to get into the work again. She felt awful, dirty and hot, and the hunger gnawed inside her. She struggled through the pile of papers in front of her and then gave up.

She ran the bath as soon as she came home. In the mirror she saw her face, grey with dust, and she grimaced at her reflection.

She washed and scrubbed and shampooed. Having dressed again, she went in search of food.

The living room was empty. A single place setting reflected a loneliness she didn't want to feel. The refrigerator held a variety of food she had not expected to find— part of a large omelette filled with onions and tomatoes, sliced avocado, a fruit salad.

It was obvious to her now that Matt had prepared the food and had been waiting for her to join him. And when she hadn't come, he had gone looking for her. A sense of guilt sneaked through her mind. She sat down at the big table and ate the cold omelette, the salad, the avocado. Ants had already found a crumb of food on the table, left by Matt, and they clustered around it, squirming in frantic activity. Feeling strangely sad and lonely, she looked around the large, empty room and wondered, when, if ever, they could stop irritating each other.

With a face predicting gloom and disaster, Kwesi served them breakfast the next morning. Matt looked questioningly at Jacqueline and she shrugged her shoulders in answer, having no idea what bothered him.

'Please, we have no more dish soap,' Kwesi said when he cleared away their dishes. He had searched everywhere in town and combed Makola Market to no avail. He had tried Omo, but the detergent made the dishes slippery and the little that was left he needed for washing clothes.

Draining the last of his coffee, Matt stood up and gave Jacqueline a lopsided grin. 'Your department,' he said.

'It's not in my job description,' she said irritably.

'I know. It has nothing to do with your job. It has something to do with the daily challenge of living in Palm Paradise. I realise that this is a problem of gigantic proportions, but a college girl like you should be able to tackle it.'

Why did he get at her like this all the time? She could cheerfully strangle him for his arrogant, presumptuous attitude.

'Go jump in the lake,' she said caustically.

He laughed and grabbed his briefcase. 'I'll see you at the office.'

She was left with Kwesi looking at her, expecting miracles, no doubt. It was not a new problem and she tried to remember what other people used to do in similar dire circumstances. She searched through her memory until she came upon the answer.

'Do we have any Key soap, Kwesi?'

He nodded and disappeared in the pantry. A moment later he came back, carrying a foot-long bar of a yellow-beige substance. It was a locally made soap, used for all cleaning purposes.

'We'll need half of that, and I want you to grate it. And see if you can get a lemon, too.' She gave him some more instructions and smiled at his doubtful face. 'To-night, when I get back from work, we'll make some super-duper dish-wash liquid.'

Everything was ready when she returned from the office. A galvanised bucket half full of water stood on the cooker, steaming. Jacqueline dumped in the grated soap, the lemon juice and the lemon peel and stirred it. It was not the coolest entertainment she could imagine and she wiped the strands of wet hair out of her face. Kwesi watched her with disapproving eyes and Jacqueline grinned at him.

'Super-duper, I promise.' As she stood stirring the beige liquid, Matt entered the kitchen, glass in hand. His eye-brows shot up as he looked from Kwesi to Jacqueline to the steaming bucket.

'What, if I may ask, are you doing?'

'Making dishwash liquid,' she said, giving him a haughty smile.

He reached for his whisky bottle. 'Well, well, a woman of many talents.'

'Certainly.' She wiped the sweat from her face and lowered the flame under the bucket.

Matt poured himself a drink, casually strolled over to the cooker and looked in the bucket at the yellowish bubbling liquid. He grimaced.

'*That* stuff is dishwash liquid? Witches' brew, if you ask me.'

Jacqueline shrugged and looked him coolly in the face. 'I didn't say I was Proctor and Gamble.'

Kwesi grinned at Matt, glad he had found someone else who didn't seem enthusiastic about the concoction in the bucket.

'We use Key soap and lemon,' he said, disgust clearly visible on his face. 'Madame says it be supah-dupah.'

'Supah-dupah my foot, but I bet it works. Where did you get that glamorous recipe?' His eyes were full of laughter and Jacqueline couldn't help smiling back at him. From the tone of his voice she knew he was not really making fun of her.

'I found it in my very secret super-duper witches' handbook.'

Matt groaned. 'That's what I was afraid of.' He took his drink and disappeared into the living room.

Giving the soap one more good stir before letting it cool, she realised she was still smiling. His face had looked nice with that laugh in his eyes. She wondered why it was always like that between them, a constant up-and-down battle. One moment everything seemed easy between them and the next they were at each other again.

Dishwash liquid was not the only shortage Jacqueline had to cope with. One of the cars had broken down and it had been at the fitter's for almost two weeks now, waiting for the magical appearance of unavailable spare parts. Office work was hampered by the shortage of transportation and Matt's impatience grew by the day. Jacqueline knew that there was no other solution but to go to Togo and get the parts in Lomé. When she discussed the matter with Matt, he seemed reluctant and frowned at her suggestion.

'I'd better go myself. It's a bloody hassle and I can't begin to explain.'

'Then don't!' she said, irritation welling up inside her. 'I'll find out myself! It's my job and I'll do it!'

'Oh, for God's sake let's not fight!' He frowned. 'You're sure you want to attempt this?'

'Positive.'

'All right then. How's your French?'

'Functional.'

'Good. You'll need a visa to get into Togo. Lomé is right at the border, by the way. You'll need a re-entry permit to get back into Ghana, and an international driver's licence.'

'Wait a minute.' Jacqueline grabbed her notebook and a pencil. 'I'll write this down.' She scribbled hastily. 'Okay, what about the car? Do I need additional insurance?'

'Yes, but you have to get permission from the Exchange Control Commission at the Bank of Ghana to get it.'

They talked for another thirty minutes about details and Matt drew a map of Lomé, Togo's capital, which wasn't more than a few main streets, with the bank and the Peugeot dealer all in the same block.

It was clear to Jacqueline that Matt had little confidence in her ability to carry out the assignment. Had it never occurred to him that maybe she wasn't quite as inexperienced as he had originally assumed? Well, one day he would find out.

She called Lisa as soon as she was back in her office.

'I have to go to Lomé on business next week. Would you like to come along for some grocery shopping?'

'Oh, yes, great! I'll leave the baby with Gladys. Are you coming back the same day?'

'Yes. I'm going for spare parts for one of our cars, but

I want to take advantage of the trip for some other stuff as well. I'm dying for a piece of cheese.'

'And apples.'

'Mushrooms.'

'Wine.'

'Ham!'

Lisa laughed. 'Oh my, am I hungry! I know a little French restaurant we can go to for lunch. They have great onion soup.'

'Fine. You lead the way. My mother used to go sometimes, but I'm not sure how much I remember.'

The major part of the week was spent in getting the papers in order. She felt like a messenger boy, running from bank to insurance company to licensing office to Togo Embassy to Ministry of Internal Affairs. She sat and waited and waited, was told to come back later, the next day, in two days.

Then finally it was all in order, and she was ready to go.

She left the house at five-thirty in the morning with the night barely gone. A grey dawn clung silently to the trees and buildings, but at six the sun would take over and a new day would start. She wasn't the only one up. Pale figures hastily walked along the streets—Hausa night-watchmen in their long white or blue robes on their way home or to their day jobs.

Lisa was ready and waiting for her and soon they were out of town, going east. There wasn't much traffic at this time of day and they enjoyed driving through the quiet countryside, which seemed strangely colourless without the intensity of the sunlight.

Lisa had brought a thermos of coffee and cookies she claimed were so healthful you wouldn't need anything else to survive but water.

'What's in it?' Jacqueline asked, looking at the cookies suspiciously.

'Groundnut paste, coconut, powdered milk, agusi seeds, sesame seeds, brewers' yeast.'

'Where did you get brewers' yeast?'

'Shipped it from the States.'

'You're crazy, Lisa Turner!' Jacqueline laughed and chewed on the cookies, which were sweet and delicious. The coffee was strong and hot.

A *tro-tro* passed them by at death-defying speed, shaking and shuddering. The lorry was overloaded with passengers hanging on for dear life to the wooden benches built in the back. The slogan on the back was painted in bright red and yellow letters and decorated with flowers. *YOU CAN SAY WHAT YOU LIKE*, it read.

'Maniac!' Lisa said hotly.

There were many of the old Bedford lorries on the roads, rebuilt to carry passengers. They always reminded Jacqueline of angry bulldogs, the grilles in front resembling bared teeth.

The sun had come up and the world had come alive. The small villages they drove through were buzzing with early morning activity and Jacqueline had to keep her attention on the road where half-naked children, goats, sheep and chickens competed for the right of way.

She was looking forward to going shopping and using her French. Two years in Switzerland had given her a good working knowledge and she had spoken it quite well.

Actually, the whole idea of going to the supermarket across the border seemed like sheer madness, she thought, but for many expatriates it was important to have the foods they were used to. Adapting to other living circumstances wasn't easy for them and for some it was impossible. For Diane, for instance. *'She went home be-*

cause she couldn't stand this place—the heat, the hassles,'
Matt had said.

But if you really loved a man, Jacqueline thought, what
did it matter that you couldn't have all the comforts and
luxuries of home? Love and companionship and true
caring were enough compensation. Or *should* be.

But then she didn't know anything about their relationship, or what it had meant to Matt and Diane.

'You look terribly serious. Something wrong?' Lisa's
voice interrupted her thoughts.

Jacqueline smiled, shaking her head. 'No, just thinking.' She hesitated briefly. 'Tell me, Lisa. Did you know
Matt's ... er ... fiancée?'

'Diane?' Lisa looked at her searchingly. 'Yes, I knew
her. Everybody knew her. She was a model, you know,
very tall, all arms and legs and masses of red hair. Very
striking.' She paused. 'She went home a while ago, didn't
she?'

Jacqueline nodded. 'She didn't like it here. Matt seems
to think this is no place for a woman. He resents me
being here. He wanted a man for the job.'

'I see. Quite a spot you're in.'

Jacqueline wanted desperately to confide in someone.
She needed a friend and she liked Lisa.

'Lisa, I....'

'He's bitter because he couldn't get Diane to stay with
him and he's taking it out on you because you happen to
be a female. If Diane can't cope with the strains and
stresses, why should you?'

'Something like that.'

'It's nonsense, of course, to think that you can't do
the job. This place crawls with working women—em-
bassies, UN, AID. They manage quite well, and so will
you.'

'I know, but he doesn't seem to think so. We're at each

other's throats constantly. . . .' Suddenly all her bitterness
came bubbling up and she clenched her hands on the
steering wheel. 'He's putting me down all the time, trying to intimidate me. How can I work with a guy like
that?' She bit her lip, afraid she'd said too much. 'I'm
sorry, Lisa, I shouldn't have said anything. I shouldn't
talk like that about my boss. Forget I said anything.'

'Sure.' Behind the large tinted glasses, Lisa's eyes were
serious, understanding. 'You just needed to talk. We all
do at times, you know.' She smiled at Jacqueline. 'Don't
worry, I'm as silent as a rock.'

The savannah stretched out between the villages and
the vegetation was dry and scarce. Here and there were
small plots of cassava plants and some sorry-looking
sugar-cane. The landscape looked bare and empty.

Closer to the border it began to look greener. Coconut
palms appeared and they could see the ocean glittering
in the distance.

It was a long, straight ride due east and they arrived
in Aflao shortly after eight. The border town was full of
activity and resembled a market place. Contraband
flourished here and everywhere there were stalls overloaded with commodities hard to find in the rest of the
country.

'Look at that,' said Lisa, pointing to a brightly coloured
kiosk.

ARISTOTLE ENTERPRISES, Jacqueline read. She
laughed. 'I love it. How can people not like a place like
this? It's full of humour and surprises.'

The Customs building stood right by the beach and
Jacqueline stayed in the car while Lisa went inside with
their passports, permits and various other papers. Past the
wire fencing Jacqueline saw the Atlantic Ocean splashing big turbulent waves on to the sandy beach. The water

glittered in the hot sun and the wind carried the smells of salt water and fish. She heard excited voices and directed her gaze to the vehicle parked next to hers.

A man was standing on top of a small blue and white bus, taking sacks and boxes handed to him by other people. He stowed them neatly and tightly on the rack and when he was finished, more men climbed up and covered the cargo with a heavy cloth. She saw them strain their muscles pulling the ropes to tie the cloth, their dark bodies on top of the car contrasting against the blue, blue sky. People shouted advice and they replied angrily. Obviously they knew what they were doing. Her eyes caught a large plastic bag lying on the ground, full of thongs, hundreds and hundreds of them in yellow, blue, red and green.

She sighed. It was stifling in the car and she wished Lisa would come back. Flies had entered the car and bothered her beyond endurance. They were big, fat and stupid and not hard to kill. If only she had something she could swat them with. She couldn't find anything. Two young girls with headpans stopped near the car and stared at her. Did she want to buy carrots? Bananas? Pineapple? No, she didn't. She wanted a fly swatter. Did they have one?

'Please, no. We have no fly swatter,' one of the girls answered, and they both giggled and walked on.

Lisa finally returned and they crossed the border and checked in at the Togolese Customs building. After that they went to the bank to get francs and Jacqueline left her parts list at the dealer's to pick up later. Lisa showed her the large new supermarket with a huge parking lot and Jacqueline looked at the place in surprise. 'Just like home. I can't believe it!'

It was wonderfully cool inside and they thoroughly

enjoyed going through the aisles of shelves stacked high with groceries imported from France and many other places.

'I never thought I'd learn to enjoy shopping.' Lisa said. 'But every time I come here it's like Christmas.'

By lunch time the car was loaded to capacity with cheese, mushrooms, cooking oil, powdered milk, frozen chickens, soap, and a hundred rolls of toilet paper.

'We'll have to get ice at the Grand Marché before we have lunch,' said Lisa, 'or the chickens and the cheese will decompose before we get home.'

The heat was oppressive in the high-roofed market and the heavy air was thick with undefinable smells. Pulling and pushing people thronged round the stalls. Women sat behind small piles of onions, tomatoes, garden eggs, chattering and laughing. One mammie was filling empty whisky bottles with groundnuts and since the price was lower here than in Accra they each bought a bottle. Imagination and creativity weren't lacking in the African character, Jacqueline thought as she looked at her purchase.

It was after one when they finally emerged from the market followed by a boy carrying the ice and a girl with a basket of vegetables on her head. The car was an oven and they quickly stuffed the rest of their purchases inside and arranged the ice in the styrofoam cooler they'd brought for the purpose.

They found the little restaurant in a side street and ordered onion soup, steak and a bottle of water. Lisa spooned away at her soup with obvious appetite until suddenly she stopped and stared into her bowl.

'What's the matter?' Jacqueline asked her.

'Look at this.' Lisa put some soup on her spoon and held it out for her to see.

'A cockroach. *Bon appetit!*'

'I don't believe I'll finish this.' Lisa calmly put her spoon down and beckoned a waiter. 'Now watch him charge me for it,' she said after the waiter had taken away her bowl.

The rest of the meal passed without incident and was tasty enough. The cockroach didn't impair their appetites.

'My mother would faint thinking about it,' said Lisa, laughing. 'These happenings make wonderful horror stories back home.'

The waiter did, indeed, charge her for the soup and had to go back to the proprietress to have the bill changed. She was a Frenchwoman with short, very straight hair, too much make-up and a loud voice. They watched her as she shouted at the waiter in rapid French.

'Poor waiters,' Jacqueline said. 'I'll bet she tyrannises the lot of them.'

Outside the heat enveloped them like a damp blanket. The car seats were so hot they had to cover them before sitting down. In minutes they were soaked with perspiration. At the Peugeot dealer's they had to wait twenty minutes to have the bill prepared and it was after three when they finally reached the border.

Jacqueline looked with trepidation at the boxes and bags in the car and groaned. 'I hope they'll let us through Customs with all this stuff.'

'Be calm and pleasant. Tell them you have a lot of kids to feed. And if they give us a bad hassle, break down in tears—works without fail. But if you get nasty, you haven't got a prayer.'

It was a lucky day and they went through without problems. Even the border guards at the check points along the road back to Accra showed a pleasant lack of interest, waving them on without checking.

It was just after dark when Jacqueline finally arrived

home, having dropped off Lisa at her house first. Matt opened the door as soon as she came up the drive.

'I'm glad you're back,' he said. 'The roads here are not made for driving after dark. Have any trouble?'

'No, everything's fine. Is Kwesi here? I have some things in the car.' She opened the door and the light inside came on. She saw his face when he looked in the car and laughed at his expression of astonishment and disbelief. Quickly he pulled his face straight and grabbed the first box off the back seat to carry it inside.

'Kwesi wasn't feeling well,' he said over his shoulder. 'He had a bad headache, so I told him to go to bed.'

She followed him to the kitchen with another box and put it down on the counter. Matt pulled a bottle out of one of the boxes and stared at it. 'Good God! Peanuts in a whisky bottle!'

Jacqueline laughed. 'I got that in the Grand Marché.'

'Well,' he commented, surveying the groceries, 'it looks like you found your way around.'

She wiped her hair away from her face and smiled. 'Lomé isn't exactly a metropolis, but it does have some very well-stocked supermarkets.'

He frowned. 'Yes, I know. But that's not why I sent you. I wanted car parts and I hope you got them. Toilet paper and mushrooms aren't exactly priorities.'

She felt a sudden sinking feeling of despair. 'I have the car parts,' she said, clenching her hands into fists. She turned away, going back to the car to get them. She put the boxes on the table, produced the list, the invoice and the receipt. 'If you'd care to check this now we'll have it over with and you won't lie awake worrying about it.' She wanted to sound cool and calm, but she heard an un-expected wobble in her voice. She turned her face away and bit her lip.

There was silence for a moment and when she turned

around she saw him looking at her, his eyes dark and unreadable.

'Sorry I mentioned it. We'll leave it till tomorrow. You're exhausted. Sit down and I'll take the rest of the stuff out of the car and fix you something to eat.'

'If I sit down now, I'll never get up again,' she sighed. 'I think I'll take a shower, if you don't mind. I'm so dirty, I can't stand myself.'

When she came back into the kitchen, Matt was breaking eggs in a bowl. 'Quite a collection of groceries you have here.' He motioned towards the counter. 'You'd better keep it out of my reach or I'll help you eat it all.'

Jacqueline stared at him. 'It's meant for both of us, of course. We're sharing the kitchen, aren't we?'

He grinned. 'I hoped you'd say that. Let me know what I owe you.'

He made an omelette with the ham and the cheese. They opened a jug of wine and had apples for dessert. It was like a rich man's feast. But two glasses of wine had Jacqueline's head reeling. Drink always went to her legs first, made them feel heavy and tired. Then it hit her head. The effect was stronger now that she was exhausted from her trip.

'One more glass and I'll be drunk,' she said. 'I'd better go to bed.'

Matt rose to his feet and held out his hand to her to pull her out of the chair. 'Not so tough when it comes to alcohol, right?'

She saw the laughter in his eyes and, for a reason she couldn't fathom, she felt embarrassed. 'It's my one and only weakness.'

He laughed out loud. Then, still holding her hand, he pulled her to him and looked down into her eyes. 'Maybe we should be drinking instead of fighting,' he said in a low voice. 'You're pretty nice tonight.'

His face was very close and his eyes held hers. She didn't move, couldn't move. Then, slowly, he bent down and his lips touched hers in a warm and tender caress. His arms moved around her and held her lightly. She stood motionless in his embrace while an unfamiliar warmth filled her being. Then, as if propelled by an unknown force, she moved closer and put her arms around his neck. The pressure of his lips became firmer and she responded, hesitantly at first, then with less restraint.

Her head was swimming, her heart pounding wildly against her ribs. A confused mixture of thoughts whirled around in the far recesses of her mind. *This is crazy*, she thought. *What's happening to me? Why is he doing this?* Never before had she reacted like this to a man's kiss. And she shouldn't now. She moved her face away, buried it against his chest. Overwhelmed by emotions, she felt weak and helpless. For a while they just stood there, silently, his arms firmly around her. Then he let her go, smiling down at her. She lowered her eyes, not wanting him to see her confusion, but he took her face in his hands and forced her to look at him.

'We do that very well together, don't we?' he said softly. 'Maybe we should try that more often. It sure beats fighting.'

She was lost for words and stared at him numbly.

'Something wrong?'

Gathering the remnants of her senses, she smiled. 'No, nothing. It's the wine. It ... it does things to me.'

An amused look came into his face. 'Yes, I know what you mean.' He released her face. 'Goodnight, Jacqueline.'

'Goodnight, Matt.'

She entered her apartment, feeling shaken and off balance. Had it actually happened? Was that Matt who had kissed her? Was that the same man who raged at her in the office, put her down, infuriated her no end?

But he had only kissed her, she thought in confusion. Nothing more. A plain old ordinary kiss. Nothing to get excited about.

But it hadn't been ordinary. Why, she didn't know, couldn't explain. Her own reactions had told her there had been more. Even now, she could still feel that strange warmth, the electric vibrations....

You've had too much wine, she told herself. Stop fantasising. Go to bed and clear your head. He was in a good mood tonight; enjoy it while it lasts.

It didn't last very long. The next morning Matt came storming into her office with undisguised fury. He threw some papers on her desk and glared at her with flames of anger leaping in his eyes.

'Well, this explains a few things!'

CHAPTER FOUR

IT took her only a glance to see that her long-lost
résumé lay on top of the papers Matt had thrown in
front of her. The rest, she assumed, were the references
and the evaluation of her interview with Christopher
Jenkins in New York. It had taken more than two
months for the papers to arrive in Accra. She looked at
Matt and saw his eyes blazing down on her.

'It explains what?' she asked.

His lips curled in contempt. 'Your miraculous adjust-
ment, your painless acclimatisation, your cultural
sensitivity. Three years in Ghana, two in Turkey and
two in Switzerland. Your French, I should think, is more
than just functional.' His voice was hard and cutting and
Jacqueline winced at the sound of it. For a moment she
said nothing. Then she shrugged her shoulders.

'Not such a green college girl, after all?'

'Why the hell didn't you tell me?'

'You didn't ask. As you may remember, you were doing all the telling.'

'Looking back, I realise I should have guessed, but I
didn't. I must have looked like a fool. I hope you're satisfied!' He marched out of the room, slamming the door
behind him.

It should have been a moment of triumph for Jacqueline, but she felt strangely deflated. The constant clashes
were getting to her. She could handle the job, but she
wasn't sure she could cope with the daily strain of working with Matt and the ever-present tension between
them.

All morning she worked with frantic intensity, trying not to let her mind wander. Her desk was piled high with reports that needed to be checked over and sent out.

She was getting more involved now with the different projects, learning about their operation from the reports and her discussions with Matt. A few times he had taken her with him on his visits, so she had a general idea of what was going on. It was interesting to know the reality that lay behind the numbers and figures and all the paper work she dealt with daily.

At twelve o'clock Matt came striding back into her office, cold and businesslike.

'I forgot to tell you, we have a guest for lunch—a guy from AID. He's been very useful to us. Will you be ready to go in ten minutes or so?'

Jacqueline nodded. 'I'm just about finished.'

'Good. Let me know when you're ready to go.'

Their guest was already waiting for them when they came home.

'Jacqueline, this is David Gordon from AID. Jacqueline Donnelly, my Administrative Assistant.'

Jacqueline stared at the tall blond man, not believing her eyes. Her mind went racing back in time—seeing David as he was then, a skinny, hungry-looking Peace Corps volunteer, eating her mother's meals with relish every time he came to Accra from his village. He was older now, more of a man. He still had the same intense blue eyes that looked at her now with obvious surprise and pleasure.

'Jackie!' He pulled her to him, giving her a big, friendly hug. 'What are you doing here, girl?'

'I'm working for Matt. Oh, it's so good to see you!'

His hands rested on her shoulders. 'Where are your parents? Here?'

'In the States. I'm on my own. I'm a big girl now, you know.'

He gave her a wide grin. 'Yes, I can see.'

Jacqueline was aware of Matt watching them. The expression in his eyes made her blush. Was he laughing at her?

David turned to Matt in an obvious attempt to draw him into the conversation. 'When I was a volunteer here I used to stay with Jackie's family when I came to town. Her mother's cooking saved me from sure starvation. I had a rotten job in the Volta region and every chance I had I came to Accra for some moral support and culinary fortification.'

'I'm sure you needed it,' Matt replied.

Kwesi brought in the meal and they sat down to eat. After the arrival of the revealing papers, Jacqueline was glad she didn't have to be alone with Matt at lunch. She said little while she ate, letting the two men talk about their business.

She was ridiculously happy to see David again. She had been a schoolgirl, seventeen, going to the International School, when David used to come to their house. Together they'd played hours of Owari, Scrabble, and gin rummy. She'd sat listening to him and watching him while he talked to her father about maize production, fishing, or the political situation. She'd had a schoolgirl crush on him, fascinated as she was with his tough, rough existence as a volunteer. His stories, sometimes heartrending, about the people he worked with in the dirty, poverty-stricken village had intrigued her and often touched her deeply.

Sometimes he'd taken her out to obscure little night clubs where high-life bands played in open courtyards. Sitting at sticky tables under tall coconut palms, they drank shandies and talked. But never once had he taken advantage of her feelings for him and often she had wondered if, indeed, he had known that she was half in love with him.

It had not been very serious. Once back in the States, wrapped up in college life, she had quickly forgotten about him. Looking at him now, she realised how long it had been. Six years. He looked infinitely more attractive now, not as hungry-looking as she remembered. Seeing his shapeless shirt of some wild and exotic African cotton, she realised his taste in clothes hadn't changed much. The more unconventional, the better. Surely he wouldn't wear that crazy thing to his office? But, knowing him, he probably did.

'You want more paw-paw?' Matt pushed a plate towards her and she met his eyes across the table. 'You're dreaming,' he said. 'I wonder about what?'

Jacqueline could feel her cheeks grow warm and her embarrassment must have been visible because he grinned at her maliciously. Then he pushed back his chair and rose to his feet. 'I'll see what's happened to the coffee.'

When he disappeared into the kitchen, David leaned forward on the table and grinned. 'I feel some very bad vibrations between the two of you.'

Jacqueline stared down at her plate, not answering.

'It's all right, Jackie, I'm not prying. But there is something I'd like to know.'

She smiled. 'Ask me.'

'Are you unattached, free, and willing to go out with me tomorrow night?'

He took her to the Palm Court, a beautiful new Chinese restaurant right on the beach. Jacqueline had never tasted better food. It seemed strange to sit here in the middle of Africa surrounded by the rich red, gold and black of

Chinese décor, eating exotic Oriental food.

She smiled at David, feeling happy and contented. He had dressed up for the occasion, wearing a bright blue bush jacket, an open-necked shirt tailored like a jacket. Matt often wore bush jackets. He had several in a variety of muted tones which she liked better than the flamboyant colours David seemed to prefer.

'You haven't changed at all,' said David, looking at her with laughter in his eyes. 'You look just like you did.'

Jacqueline groaned. 'Yes, like an eighteen-year-old college freshman.'

'What's wrong with looking like a sexy eighteen-year-old?'

'For one thing, people don't hire sexy eighteen-year-olds for the kind of job I was looking for. I was *serious*, and nobody believed me.'

'You didn't do so badly. IFP has quite a good reputation.'

'Do you know how long it took me to find this job? I was turned down a dozen times, and not because of lack of qualifications, I assure you. Employers took one look at me and wrote me off as a dumb blonde. For some reason or other, my qualifications didn't do a thing to counteract that impression.'

'It must be a terrible burden to be blonde and beautiful.' There was no doubt about the laughter in his eyes.

'Oh, stop it, David! You're not taking me seriously! That's my whole trouble, you see. Even Matt....' She bit her lip, not finishing her sentence.

'Even Matt what?'

'Never mind. Forget it.'

'I'm sorry I upset you,' he said, smiling. 'Tell me about your parents and what they're doing.'

Safe subject, Jacqueline thought, pouring more tea.

'They're at home right now. They bought a house in

Maine and they'll be there for a couple of years while my father is writing a book on development. I suppose they'll go overseas again after it's finished.'

'What made you decide to come to Ghana?'

'Oh, I always wanted to come back and work. I liked it here and. . . .' She hesitated, stopped.

'And what?'

She felt a little uncomfortable. It wasn't easy to talk about her feelings. Most people didn't understand, thought she was some kind of misguided idealist.

'Well, you know. . . . I've always had everything I needed in life and a lot more and . . . well, I guess it's silly, but I've always felt uneasy about it. I mean, why me? Why did I deserve all this while so many people in the world are suffering one way or another.' She stared at her plate. 'I wanted to do something.'

'I see,' he said quietly, 'so you came to Africa to soothe your conscience. Instead of sending your ten dollars to the Society for the Blind, you're doing your thing here.'

Jacqueline stared at him in shocked horror. Then anger flooded through her. 'David! That's a terrible thing to say! How could you!'

He was not taken aback in the slightest.

'It's not true, then?'

'No, it is not! If all I wanted to do was clear my conscience, I wouldn't have had to come all the way over here. I could have stayed right in the States. There are a few disadvantaged people left there I could have bestowed my benevolent favours on!' She paused. 'One reason I came to Africa was because I like the place and the people. I enjoy the international atmosphere and meeting interesting people. A very selfish reason, if I may point that out. And yes, I am grateful for the advantages I've had—good care, loving parents, an education. And I do feel I want to share this and do something that might help people who are less fortunate than I am. There's no one single reason why I came here. It all just came together this way.' Jacqueline stopped, out of breath. She didn't look at him, but picked up her fork and fiercely stabbed a sweet and sour shrimp.

'I've upset you,' he observed wryly.

'Yes, you have! I thought you knew me better than that.'

'I didn't. You were sweet, sixteen—seventeen when I knew you last. Nice, and fun, and pretty sharp, but not altogether straightened out in the head, if I may say so.'

Jacqueline said nothing to this. He was right, of course. At seventeen life has its questions, and for her there had been plenty. But that was six years ago and since then she'd figured some of them out.

'Jackie, look at me.'

She lifted her eyes from the shrimp on her plate, saw his blue, blue eyes, felt her anger melting away.

'I wanted to know your motivations,' he said. 'I'm sorry if my tactics were a little straight and strong. Am I forgiven?' His smile was disarming.

'All right,' she said, smiling back at him.

'There's only one thing. Don't make the mistake I made as a volunteer.'

'Oh?'

'I got in way too deep. That's easy when you live in a village and know everyone personally and become involved in their lives. I got terribly emotional about it all and lost all perspective in the end. It's counter-productive. I caused myself a lot of heartache and didn't accomplish very much. . . .'

He looked a little sad and she remembered the David of six years ago, struggling with the projects in the village, his desperation, his anger.

'You sound disillusioned,' she commented.

'I was, and still am, in a way. It took me a couple of years after I went back to the States to pull myself together.'

'And here you are, back again.'

'But I learned my lesson. No more emotional involvements. Everything businesslike, calm and cool, straight down the line.'

'Now you sound like a cynic. Surely there must be some middle ground?'

David shrugged. 'I'm trying to be practical and rational. And I wanted to warn you.'

'I don't think my job will get me too close to the emotional side of things,' said Jacqueline. She felt a little disappointed. David wasn't the same as she remembered. Some of the eagerness and enthusiasm had gone out of him. Now he was just doing a job, that was all. No doubt he was doing his work well, but he was doing it with his mind, not with his heart.

He smiled at her across the table. 'We're much too serious.' He took her hand. 'Come along, let's go for a walk on the beach.'

They took off their shoes and walked barefoot on the hard, wet sand along the water. Jacqueline's long skirt flapped around her ankles, and she felt wonderful, carefree, happy. I'm always on guard, she thought. That's why. I'm always worrying and wondering what Matt's going to say or do next. Well, she didn't want to think about him now.

There was nothing but the sound of the waves roaring in the distance, rolling towards the beach, splashing at their feet. The white foam glowed strangely in the light of the moon. The ocean at her feet and the stars far off in the distant sky made her feel small and insignificant.

'Intimidating, isn't it?' commented David, as if he had read her thoughts. They walked hand in hand for a long time, not saying much, just enjoying the peaceful serenity around them.

Then suddenly David dropped his shoes in the sand and stepped in front of her. She stood still, looking up into his face, and she saw him smile.

'I'm an incurable romantic,' he said, and wrapped his arms tightly round her and kissed her.

She kissed him back. It was a romantic evening and David was a nice man and she liked his arms around her.

'Mmmm, that was nice,' he said, as he let her go. 'Let's go skinny-dipping,' he added suddenly, and she had to laugh at the enthusiasm in his voice.

'No way! I'm much too inhibited.'

'Really?'

'Really.'

'Well, I didn't really think you would. You've always been an old-fashioned sort of a girl, haven't you?' He squeezed her hand and in the light of the moon she could see him smile.

It was after midnight when he dropped her off at home.

'Thanks, David, I've had a wonderful evening.'

'Me too.' He leaned over and kissed her lightly. 'We'll do it again soon. And don't forget your swimsuit!'

She lay in bed thinking about David, about their walk on the beach. What had he said after he had kissed her? *That was nice.* Yes, it had been nice, and that was the whole trouble. That had always been the trouble. Nice just wasn't enough. Something was missing. There was no sparkle, no electricity. She turned over, pulling the sheet closer around her. Was she just hoping for something unrealistic, something that didn't exist outside romantic novels? But it did exist. She knew it. She had felt it, hadn't she? Not so very long ago. The night she had come back from Togo when Matt had kissed her goodnight it had been there—the sparkle, the electricity. But she'd had too much wine, and it had meant nothing. After all, Matt wasn't exactly one of her favourite people.

The men she had known had been good men, friendly, dependable, interesting, courteous. But none of them had ever stirred her deeper feelings. *Because you want too much*, she told herself. What else do you want besides good and dependable and nice? Isn't it enough? *No, it isn't enough*, she thought desperately.

She wanted to fall in love, madly in love. She wanted a man who would totally throw her off her equilibrium, who'd make her drunk with happiness, whose touch would send shivers down her spine, whose smile would make her heart start racing.

She sighed, staring up at the ceiling. Men like that didn't exist. Love just wasn't like that in real life, that all-consuming, all-important emotion young girls dreamed of.

It's time you grew up, she told herself. And with a sense of loss and sadness she fell asleep.

Lack of male companionship wasn't one of Jacqueline's problems. A single girl in a town like Accra had no shortage of invitations from eager young men who wanted to take her dining and dancing. But she preferred to spend most of her free time with David. They went swimming or dancing or to the open-air cinemas. Sitting under starry skies they saw every half-way passable movie that came to town.

Although she enjoyed David's company, she would notice time and again how much he really had changed. Rarely did he mention his work. The enthusiasm that had been so much a part of him had vanished. Whenever someone drew him into a conversation about his work, or development in general, he was cynical and pessimistic. It hurt her to listen to him and she avoided the subject. She didn't agree with him, but she had no defences against his negativism.

On occasion she would accept an invitation from someone else—a German anthropologist, an Italian diplomat. But sometimes she received more entertainment than she had bargained for.

One night she had a particularly frustrating experience keeping a rather persistent young Lebanese man at a comfortable distance. When she finally made it home she was bursting with anger. She flung her wrap on a chair and stormed into the kitchen for a glass of cold water, colliding with Matt, who grabbed her by the arms and steadied her.

'Well, what's all this agitation about? Are you mad?'

'I most certainly am!'

'What have I done now?' His eyes were full of amusement as he looked down on her.

'Nothing—this time. I'm mad at this Kahlil what's-his-name—he was in the office to see you last week.' She took a bottle of cold water from the refrigerator and poured herself a drink.

Matt's eyebrows shot up. 'Oh, yes, that character.' Then he grinned. 'Can't cope with that fiery Arabic temperament?'

'I don't know about that. I only know that he has some very strange ideas about Western women.'

'You didn't make it particularly easy for him, did you?' His eyes moved slowly, lazily down the length of her body and Jacqueline gritted her teeth in anger.

'What, if I may ask, do you mean by that?'.

'Look at the way you're dressed,' he said calmly, dispassionately.

She glanced down at the slinky lavender and blue dress reaching to the floor. It was a pretty dress and it fitted her well, but she couldn't for the world see what he was talking about.

'What's wrong with the way I'm dressed?'

She caught the gleam of mockery in his eyes.

'You don't leave much to the imagination, do you?'

'I'm quite adequately covered from shoulders to ankles!' she answered hotly.

'Makes no difference,' he said, his mouth faintly curved at the corners.

'What am I suposed to do? Wrap a tent around me and pretend I weigh two hundred pounds?'

'Oh, come on now,' he said soothingly, taking the glass from her hand. 'Don't get mad at me now. I know how much you like to fight, but one battle a night ought to be enough.' He put the glass down in the sink and leaned lazily against the counter. 'You know, with a social life like yours you'd better save your strength.'

Rage burned inside her and she glared at his long frame, his laughing face. He was waiting for her to say something, to burst out in fury; she could see his expectation in his eyes. Well, she wasn't going to! With a strength she didn't know she possessed, she steadied her nerves, straightened her face and smiled at him.

'You're so right. Goodnight, Matt.' Without giving him another look, she walked out of the kitchen.

'I wish I could get a flat somewhere else,' she mumbled furiously to herself, kicking off her shoes. Then at least she could go home at night and eat by herself and not run into him every time she went to the kitchen. She saw quite enough of him during the day. But finding a flat was impossible and she knew it. And actually, she liked this place. It was just right for her, small and intimate with its bright curtains, pillows and paper lampshades she'd brought from home. Lisa had given her a round straw mat she didn't need any more and it looked nice on the wooden floor. The furniture had been made by a roadside carpenter and it was basic and simple, which Jacqueline liked.

Sighing, she began to take off her clothes. She walked into the bathroom and turned on the shower. In the few short months she'd been here she'd already grown attached to her own place. She liked sitting on the little verandah reading or writing or just watching the lizards chase each other. After the gardener had come back from his village, Jacqueline had asked him not to cut back the bougainvilleas and he had obliged, somewhat unwillingly. After all, this was *his* garden and *he* was the gardener. He obviously took great pride in his work. Jacqueline sometimes watched him as he cut the grass with his hand-sickle, muscles rippling under the shiny brown skin of his bare back.

He always brought his little daughter with him so she could play with Kwesi's little girl. She loved watching them as they ran through the garden, chasing Kwesi's chickens, laughing and screaming. Jacqueline was fascinated by the games they played and the imagination they demonstrated. There was no television to entertain them and they had virtually no toys. Still they never showed any signs of boredom. Once Jacqueline had bought each of them a cheap plastic doll in Makola market and their delight had been touching.

The water was too hot. With her toe she turned the cold water tap a little. That felt good. She stood under the shower for a long time, thinking. There was another solution : she could simply quit. Tell Christopher Jenkins that she liked the job, but not the boss. Matt would be delighted, she was quite sure.

She stepped out of the shower and dried herself off. Of course, going home was not a real alternative. She had no intention of giving up. She liked Ghana. She liked her job. She just couldn't stand Matt Simmons.

'We'd better get moving if we want to make the party at six.'

Jacqueline had been so absorbed in her work that she hadn't heard Matt come into her office. She looked up, surprised to see him standing in front of her.

'Party? What party?'

He frowned. 'The cocktail party at the Jurgensons',' he said with an impatient gesture.

She knew nothing about it, and she had no desire to go. Another hour or so and she would have this insurance business straightened out. She wanted to do it now.

'I know nothing about it. I didn't get an invitation.'

'Well, no matter. You're coming anyway. Let's get going.'

So he was trying to order her around in her free time too, was he? It wasn't enough to work with him all day, to live in his house, eat her meals with him. Now he wanted her to accompany him to social functions as well. Sparks of rebellion exploded inside her.

'I'm not going,' she said as calmly as she could manage.

A cocktail party wasn't what she needed now. Standing around with a glass of something-or-other in your hand, listening to the women complain about servants and shortages, wasn't her idea of a good time.

Matt placed both hands on her desk and leaned towards her, looking at her with brows raised.

'Oh, you are not? May I ask you why?'

'I told you, I didn't get an invitation and I intend to have a splitting headache tonight.' She waved her hand in a casual gesture. 'Migraine, isn't that what it's called?'

He came closer and his eyes bored into hers. 'I'm in no mood for little girl games,' he said, his voice dangerously low. 'You'll come to the party with me because it's a business assignment.'

A sudden sense of recklessness surged through her.

'And what will you do if I don't comply with your wishes? Fire me?'

He straightened, thrusting his hands into his pockets. For a long moment he stared at her, his eyes dark and ominous. 'I have no such intention,' he said slowly.

She raised her brows. 'You don't? Surprise, surprise! I thought you were anxious to get rid of me.'

'I'm not in the habit of firing employees who perform well on the job.' It was a statement of fact and not meant as a compliment, she was fully aware of that.

'Not even a female?' She couldn't resist the question. His face was hard and angry, but she didn't avert her eyes.

'You won't let me forget it, will you?' he muttered between clenched teeth. 'Well, let me tell you this, little girl. It's brains, competence and stamina I care about, not sex! You could be a dinosaur, for all I care! Just so the job gets done!'

His rage suddenly made her want to laugh, but she checked the impulse.

'Well, I'm a sucker for compliments,' she said mockingly. 'Makes me weak as butter.'

Their eyes met for a long moment, but neither one said a word. Then Matt turned and walked to the door.

'I'm going home now,' he flung over his shoulder. 'I expect you to be ready at ten to six.'

But she wasn't ready. She stood in her bra and panties in front of her bathroom mirror putting on her make-up, when she heard his knock on the connecting door. Let

him wait, she thought rebelliously, ignoring the knock.
All she had to do was put on her earrings, slip her long
dress over her head and put her shoes on.

A moment later the half open bathroom door swung
open farther. There was a faint hint of aftershave. Her
frightened glance took in Matt, dressed in beige pants
and a neat, well-fitting bush jacket in a mixture of
browns. He stood on the threshold, surveying her with
calculated appraisal.

'Well, well. Leave it to a female not to be ready on
time!'

'You noticed?' It wasn't easy to stay calm under his
unperturbed gaze. She could tell him to leave, of course,
but he'd only laugh and she didn't want to give him the
satisfaction. She picked up her earrings and started putting one in, ignoring him and the little ripples of uneasiness surging through her. If he wants to embarrass
me, he'll have to be more original, she thought angrily,
pulling on her earlobe. Her hands were trembling and
she had trouble putting the post through the hole. She
dropped the ring into the sink and she was aware of him
standing there, laughing at her. She bit her lip and concentrated once more on her earlobe in the mirror.

'Am I making you nervous?'

'No!'

He laughed out loud at the obvious untruth of her
angry reply. He folded his arms and leaned against the
doorpost.

'If you were a virtuous little girl, you'd tell me to
leave. You're not dressed for male visitors.'

'I'm sure you've seen women dressed in less than this,
but if it shocks you, by all means remove yourself and
wait in the sitting-room.'

'I'm rather enjoying this, actually.' He shifted his position, but made no move to go.

Her earlobe was red now and she knew she wasn't going to get the blasted earring in, not with her fingers trembling as they did.

'Here, let me help you.' His hand was on her shoulder and instantly she whirled around, avoiding his touch.

'Get out!'

He shook his head. 'Not yet. You look much too inviting dressed in next to nothing.' His arms shot out and he grabbed her by the shoulders. 'You're trembling,' he said softly, his eyes full of amusement. 'Don't worry, I don't have murder on my mind.' He pulled her against him and she wanted to strike out at him, but she was helpless in his grip. His kiss was forceful, yet tender, his hands strong and warm on the bare skin of her back. She went limp in his arms, her lips parting in response.

I can't let this happen, she thought in sudden panic, her mind still struggling, if not her body. I can't just give in to him as soon as he touches me....

His hands stroked her back, moved up and he entwined his fingers in her hair, pulling the pins loose. His lips left hers and he kissed her closed eyes and the softness of his caress sent a shiver through her. Her mind went blank of thought and all awareness of time and place left her.

Her legs were weak when he released her and he gave her a strange, lopsided smile. 'It even works without alcohol. How about that?'

Sanity returned and with it a sense of shame and deep anger. She turned away from him, gripping the sink with both hands to steady herself.

'Leave me alone! And get out!'

'Yes, ma'am,' he said meekly, but she noticed his reflection in the mirror. He was biting his lip and there was laughter in his eyes. He turned and carefully closed the door behind him.

Jacqueline sank down on the edge of the bathtub, still

trembling. Why did he do this to her? Did he realise the
effect he had on her? Did he use it to get even, show her
he was boss no matter what the circumstances?

She stood up and with shaky fingers began to brush
out her hair and put it back on top of her head. Somehow, she got in the earrings and then went into the bedroom to put on her clothes. The long, sweeping skirt of
her new dress made her look taller than she was and the
brown and golds of the African print material went well
with her hair. She'd made the dress herself, using Lisa's
sewing machine, and she was pleased with the results.

Apparently so was Matt. He whistled approvingly
when she entered the sitting-room, but she ignored it and
walked past him in icy silence.

Neither of them said a word during the short ride to
the Jurgensons' house. The party was outside, lit up by
electric bulbs placel in strategic locations. Under the
palms and mango trees, people stood talking in small
groups, glasses in their hands. Matt introduced her all
around and she tried hard to remember the names of the
Ghanaian and American businessmen and government
officials. After a while he left her to do some circulating
on her own and she enjoyed herself a great deal talking
to Mr Fordwor, a handsome Ghanaian businessman. Mr
Fordwor travelled extensively, mostly to Europe and the
Middle East, and he had a whole repertoire of amusing
stories about his adventures abroad.

As she moved around, she met a variety of interesting
people, and once in a while she caught sight of Matt, one
hand in his pants pocket, the other holding a drink. Talking and listening, he looked serious most of the time, and
it was obvious that he hadn't come for socialising purposes, but was using the opportunity to talk business.

Matt. She wished she weren't so terribly aware of him,
of the way he moved, the way he held his head, where

he was and whom he was talking to. Alone for the moment, she found herself staring at him. Suddenly, as if he had felt her gaze, he turned his head. Their eyes met and he smiled at her. Abruptly she turned, ignoring him, not smiling back.

A moment later he was standing in front of her.

'Still mad at me?'

So he had noticed she'd ignored him. Well, what *did* he think? Had he expected her to forgive and forget his outrageous behaviour as if it were nothing? She was mad all right, and she intended to stay that way for a while. She gave him an icy look.

'I don't go for that forceful he-man stuff.'

He took a sip of his drink and looked at her calmly.

'You were asking for it.'

'*Asking* for it? Of all the....'

'You may not be much size-wise, but your shape leaves nothing to be desired. You should know better than to stand there half naked in front of a man.'

Jacqueline clenched her teeth in fury. 'I was in my *own* bathroom, and I didn't exactly invite you in!'

'You didn't exactly send me away either,' he bounced back. 'Not until I made a pass at you.'

She had no reply to this and he laughed at her helpless anger. He took her arm. 'Come on, I'll get you another drink. Maybe that'll help you simmer down.'

'Let go of me! I'll get my own drink!' She jerked her arm away.

Suddenly he sighed. 'For God's sake, Jacqueline, do you have to make such a big deal out of nothing? Where's your sense of humour! You act as if I'd raped you. If I remember correctly, you didn't put up much of a struggle.'

Jacqueline's face grew warm with embarrassment.

'You had no right to ... to barge into my bathroom like that!'

For a long moment he looked at her silently, his eyes dark and unreadable. 'All right,' he said at last, 'I apologise.'

She stared at him in amazement, at a loss for words. Matt's face was expressionless. 'Well,' he said, 'may I get you that drink now?'

She nodded. 'Yes ... yes, please. Gin and tonic.'

Matt stalked away and she looked at his tall frame disappearing in the crowd. She still couldn't quite believe what she'd heard. For some reason she hadn't expected Matt to apologise for anything, ever.

'Do you have to make such a big deal out of nothing? Where's your sense of humour? You act as if I'd raped you.' His words echoed in her mind and suddenly she felt small and childish. Had she over-reacted? But he *had* apologised, hadn't he?

But now that she thought about it some more, she knew that Matt must be that special kind of man who could apologise and still come out the winner....

Around her people stood in groups talking and laughing, fragments of their conversations floating through the air, reaching her ears. '... carried that python on the plane in her handbag....' '... jam and soap? Where?' '... picked it up in Singapore....'

Matt came back with her drink, took her to meet some other people, and a little later left her again to talk to someone. Moving around some more, she suddenly found herself face to face with David. He put his arm around her shoulders, giving her a flashy smile.

'Hi there! Didn't know you were here.'

'Wasn't supposed to be. Gate crashed on boss's orders.'

He grinned. 'Don't let the Ambassador hear it—he'll

have you deported! Well, let me introduce you.'

She shook hands and tried to remember names, which was a hopeless endeavour from point one. There was a visiting professor from Holland, a Ghanaian surgeon, an English librarian.

'We were discussing Schnapps,' David informed her.

Jacqueline wrinkled her nose. 'Terrible stuff!'

'The professor is shocked to hear the Dutch are responsible for introducing it to Ghanaian society.'

The professor, a mousy little man, smiled weakly.

'Dey tell me it was used as a medicinal potion.'

'It tastes like one, Jacqueline agreed.

'It's supposed to cure everything,' David said. 'Gout, stomach cramps, hangnails....'

'Broken bones,' the librarian added.

'It does,' the surgeon said gravely.

They all looked at him in astonishment and then he smiled. There was an unmistakable twinkle in his eyes.

'You drink enough of that brew and you'll feel just wonderful, I assure you.'

There was a roar of laughter.

Later, Matt came looking for her and together they said goodbye to their hosts.

'It looked as if you were having a good time,' Matt observed as he manoeuvred the car out of the parking lot. 'Interesting conversation?'

'Oh, yes, very. All about booze.'

He gave her a quick, sideways glance. 'Sounds fascinating,' he said drily.

'Better than the women's conversations! Nothing but complaints about lazy servants, food shortages and the crummy weather! I'm always tempted to tell them to quit complaining or go home if they don't like it here.' As soon as she spoke the words she could feel him stiffen beside her.

'I see.' His mouth was a straight, hard line. His eyes were fixed on the road ahead of him and he didn't look at her. She realised she'd said something wrong. Of course, Diane. She'd done exactly that—gone home because she didn't like it here. Her remark hadn't been very tactful and she regretted it now.

'I'm sorry, I didn't mean to sound so self-righteous.'

He gave her a lopsided smile. 'Never mind. You're quite right, you know.'

They were quiet for a few minutes. Matt moved round Redemption Circle and continued on the ring road, speeding up a little. Then he looked at her.

'I know I introduced you to quite a number of people tonight, but do you remember Mr Minyila? The tall man in the blue robe?'

She nodded, remembering the robe. It had been elaborately embroidered, marking its wearer as a man from the north of the country.

'Is he the one who just came back from Kansas State University with a Doctorate in Agriculture?' she asked.

'Yes, that's the one.'

'He told me he's the son of a chief in the north.'

'Yes.' Matt swore and stepped on the brakes, barely missing a taxi that suddenly swerved in front of him.

'He was in my office a few weeks ago,' he continued. 'You weren't in, so you didn't meet him then. He's interested in starting a soybean project in his father's village and from what he told me, it sounds as if it's worth looking into. He wants me to come to the north and look around and talk to his father and the village elders. He repeated the invitation this evening, and I've decided I'd like to have a look. The guy intrigues me, and I'm sure he's serious about it.' He shrugged. 'Just a feeling it might be something.'

'It's quite a long way to go on a hunch,' Jacqueline said.

'Yes. But I can combine it with some other business on the way back.' His gaze settled on her face. 'How would you like to come along?'

His suggestion took her by surprise and she stared at him. 'You want me to come along? Why?'

'Well, Steven is totally wrapped up with the goats for the next few weeks, and I think you could be quite useful to me. I'd like you to take notes and write up a report on our findings there. And if it's worth it, I'll want you to do research on some more facts and figures.'

She sat silently digesting this and didn't answer him immediately. It sounded interesting. It would get her more involved with the actual work of the agency and that idea appealed to her. What was really behind all this? Was Matt suddenly realising she had some capabilities and wanting to make use of them? It was true that he had been quite positive about her work performance.

'I'd love to go,' she said, 'if you think I could help.'

They turned into their street and Ali came running from across the street where he'd been visiting his friend and flung open the gates to let the car in.

'It won't be easy, though,' said Matt, opening the door and letting her into the house. 'We'll need the car to get to the village, so we can't fly to Tamale. I want to do it at the end of the month. And I want to drive up in one day.'

'To Tamale in *one* day?'

'Think you can make it?'

She quickly recovered. 'Me? Oh, sure. I'm wondering about the car.'

He opened the door to her flat and laughed. 'Let's leave the car to Allah!'

CHAPTER FIVE

THEY started out at the ungodly hour of five, after a sleepy-eyed Kwesi had served them breakfast. It was still dark outside and relatively cool. Not much traffic was on the road yet, but that would soon change.

'Have you ever been to the north before?' Matt asked.

'Yes, with my parents, a couple of times. And with a Dutch school friend once. Her parents were missionary doctors and they lived near Bolgatanga.' Jacqueline laughed. 'We went by *tro-tro* part of the way, and the rest we hitch-hiked.'

Matt shook his head. 'Well, safer here than at home.'

'I wouldn't dream of hitch-hiking at home.'

'I bet you wouldn't. In certain respects African society is a helluva lot more civilised than the Western world.'

'One of the reasons I like it here.'

His eyes rested on her for a moment, then returned to the road. 'You really do like it here, don't you?'

Jacqueline nodded. 'Yes, especially the people. They're so happy and friendly. Europeans have always been so derogatory about Africans, but it's good to see people who are so proud of themselves and have so much self-respect.'

On the other side of the road a rickety lorry came towards them. *LIFE HAS NO SPARE PARTS*, it said in curly red and blue letters. Jacqueline laughed. 'And they're such philosophers! Look at that *tro-tro*.'

The sun had come up, bathing the world in a soft golden glow that would soon change into a bright, brilliant blaze. The road to Kumasi was heavily travelled and the tarmac showed serious signs of wear and tear. It was a job to avoid the cracks and potholes in the road, although most of the vehicles seemed to take little notice and drove at top speed, rattling and shuddering.

The hills were lush and green and covered with forest. Jacqueline enjoyed watching the scenery and looking at the villages they passed through. Small buildings of crumbling concrete with rusty corrugated iron roofs sat beside traditional mud huts with palmfrond roofs. In the shade of mango trees women sat on low stools preparing food or feeding infants. Laundry lay spread out on the ground to dry. In one of the villages an old man, all dressed up in a colourful Adinkra cloth flung over one shoulder, stood by the road, staring at the vehicles passing by. In his lifetime he must have seen more change than Jacqueline could begin to comprehend.

Jacqueline was silent with awe when they reached the Nkawkaw escarpment. Fog drifted over the sheer stone cliff, creating a dramatic view.

'Magnificent, isn't it?' Matt asked.

'It's beautiful. I could look at it all day.'

They were silent again and a while later she noticed a horse and wagon coming down the road. A decrepit-looking taxi sat on top of the blue-painted cart.

'Very symbolic,' Matt said, smiling. 'Progress sometimes takes a beating. It isn't always the modern and efficient equipment that wins the game.'

'Tell me about this village,' she said. 'You haven't told me much.'

'I don't know that much. Mr Minyila gave me the distinct impression, though, that the whole village is involved in this project. He told me that a few years ago they built a clinic all by themselves with local material and on their own initiative. And then they pushed the government until they had a staff. There's a German missionary doctor there now and some Peace Corps nurses.'

'Sounds impressive.'

Matt nodded. 'Yes, and that's what gave me the idea that we may have some real possibilities. The people have seen their initiative and work pay off before. And you can't do much without that. You have to have the people with you or you can't make a project work.'

He gave her a quick, sideways glance. 'You know, Jacqueline, it isn't the rice plantation or the goat farm that cause the major problems in this kind of work. It's the people themselves—their worries, their preconceived ideas, their relationships with each other and the project sponsors.' He paused slightly, not looking at her. 'You can have all the money in the world, all the expertise, all the equipment, all the government support to set up some major enterprise, but if you haven't got the local people involved in heart, body and soul, it'll be a disaster. We've seen it all over Africa many times. Americans and Europeans think we have all the answers. We often treat the Africans like children, as if we know what's best for them. First the missionaries, then the colonialists, then the developers. And it doesn't work. It doesn't work.' Matt stared straight ahead of him, eyes fixed on the road.

Jacqueline studied his face, saying nothing.

'The Western attitude has always been: "I want to help you, so you listen and I'll tell you what to do." It's stupid and pretentious. You wouldn't talk like that to your friends. You say: "I want to help you. Tell me what you want me to do." ' He let out a sigh. 'There I go again! I'm sorry.'

Jacqueline had never seen him like this before and she was a little taken aback by his show of emotions.

He looked at her sideways. 'Do I sound like a maniac?'

'No....' She hesitated. 'You have strong feelings about

your work, that's the way I'd put it.'

He grinned. 'Very diplomatic!'

'Would you like some water?' Jacqueline asked, changing the subject.

'Yes, please.'

They had brought a big canteen full of water and ice cubes and as she awkwardly balanced cup and canteen she spilled some and felt the icy water trickle down her leg.

'Sorry, I should have slowed down more.'

'Never mind, it feels good. It's awfully hot already.'

'It'll get a lot worse,' he said, gulping down the water.

They had an early lunch in Kumasi and left as soon as possible to catch the Yeji ferry across the Volta Lake.

The lake village was bustling with activity, even at midday in scorching heat. The ferry was half-way across the lake and it wouldn't take more than an hour to get on it. Private cars had priority and a long line of trucks stood baking in the sun waiting for an available space. Some of the trucks had been there for days and the drivers had camped out underneath their lorries. Some of them were sleeping there now in the only shade available. Here and there a goat had joined them, seeking refuge from the burning sun.

Matt inched the car carefully past the long line of lorries, avoiding children and livestock wandering around in blessed oblivion. The villagers had set up their stalls and tables, loaded with food, pottery, baskets and an assortment of other goods. Matt parked the car in line and they climbed out to stretch their legs. Jacqueline could feel the sweat trickling down her body, front and back, and her dress stuck to her skin. She pulled her scarf off and retied it. Her head ached with heat and exhaustion. Even her glasses helped little against the blinding sun. Matt took out his handkerchief, mopped his face and let out a sigh.

'Life in the tropics is so exotic and exciting,' he said with mockery in his voice. 'If only people knew!'

They walked to the water's edge and they could see the ferry coming slowly across the lake. On the banks, brightly painted fishing boats lay waiting for their next trip out. Women were washing clothes, beating them on rocks to get them clean. A little girl with a shallow pan full of bananas on her head came towards them. She looked at them, stopped, and stared. Her eyes were huge and she had a dead serious expression on her face. In seconds she was surrounded by more children who looked at them silently, or pointed and giggled.

'They're all staring at you,' Matt said. 'I'll bet they've never seen an Obruni with hair as blonde as yours.' He winked at the children and they all screamed in laughter. Jacqueline had seen him play this game before. For some reason, winking was considered extremely funny, and wherever he went, Matt would wink at the children and make them laugh.

'Did anyone ever wink back at you?' she asked.

'Never. They stare or laugh or scream.'

'They think you're a weirdo doing crazy things with your eyes.'

'That's why I do it.'

'You like giving people the wrong impression of yourself?'

'Is that what I'm doing? Did I give you the wrong impression?' His eyes were laughing down on her. 'I'm not quite such a bad guy as you thought at first? Chauvinistic, prejudiced, ill-tempered, bad-mannered, etcetera, etcetera?'

'I haven't decided yet.'

His face collapsed in mock disappointment. 'Well,

maybe I'll convince you yet. I'm really quite wonderful, given half a chance.'

'I'd love to see a demonstration.' As soon as the words were out she realised their dubious content and she could feel the colour rush to her cheeks. Matt looked at her and laughed heartily, making her blush even more.

'I didn't mean. . . .' she stammered.

'I know what you didn't mean,' he said, still laughing. 'Your tongue gets ahead of your thoughts sometimes. Very dangerous!'

Mercifully the ferry had arrived and it was time to get back to the car. Throngs of pedestrians walked ashore, carrying bundles, baskets and babies. Then the cars followed and soon it was their turn to drive slowly on to the ferry, following the instructions of a man stripped to the waist, gesturing and shouting with what seemed an over-supply of energy.

They were followed by a *tro-tro* with the slogan *SWEET NOT ALWAYS*.

It seemed as if the day would never end. Her whole body ached with heat and exhaustion. The road was badly paved and sometimes not paved at all and they were constantly bouncing up and down. The breeze through the open windows was heavy with dust and carried little refreshment.

It was after six and already dark when they finally drove up to the Catering Resthouse in Tamale. Jacqueline barely had the energy to unglue herself from her seat and hoist herself out of the car.

No one was to be found at the reception desk and it took a while before Matt had rounded up a sleepy-faced young man who mumbled excuses, then leafed through the book from front to back, unable to find their reservations. Jacqueline looked at Matt. Exasperation was clearly visible on his face. How tired he looked! And how tired she felt herself. She had no feelings in her legs and her head seemed ready to fall off at any moment. A shower, then a bed, was all she wanted.

'Oh, here,' the young man said finally, clearly relieved. 'International Food Production. Bungalow 26. Two nights.'

'We have reservations for two,' Matt said irritably. 'Two rooms, sir. One for me, and one for the lady here.'

The man grinned sheepishly and studied the book some more. 'There's only one reservation here,' he said, looking up at them with a blank stare. 'But the bungalow has two beds.'

'Well, we need another room,' said Matt, exasperated.

A hunted look came into the young man's eyes. 'Please, we're full up, sir. There's the church conference in town. But tomorrow....'

'I need a room tonight!' Matt's face was tight with restrained fury and he looked more exhausted than ever. 'And I would like to see the manager, please,' he added, his voice suddenly dangerously cold and calm.

'The manager has travelled, sir.'

Jacqueline was afraid Matt was going to explode, but he didn't answer. For a moment it was quiet and when he turned around to look at her, his face was a mask of fatigue and resignation.

'Okay, we'll just have to share the bungalow. With the church conference in town, the missionary resthouse will be full too.'

Apprehension took hold of her. Sharing a room with Matt, having him sleep in the bed next to hers? The idea conjured up all manner of possibilities in her mind. It was asking for trouble. The scene in the bathroom had not left her memory, and she wondered if Matt would try to take advantage of the situation if they shared the same room for the night.

He frowned as he looked at her. 'For heaven's sake, don't look as if I'd made an indecent proposal,' he said irritably. 'You're not a nun, are you?'

She flushed, wondering whether he'd guessed her thoughts. No, she wasn't a nun, and he wasn't exactly a monk, either. That was the point, wasn't it?

'I like my privacy,' she said, feeling a little silly, but she had to say something. Obviously, liking privacy was irrelevant in this situation. There was no choice.

'Privacy is a luxury you'll have to do without. What we need is a bed and a night's rest. I'll be damned if I'm going to camp out in the car all night because you're a prude. There's a perfectly good bed available and I intend to sleep in it!' He turned around, inviting no more discussion, and there was nothing she could do but follow him to the bungalow.

It was a shabby little cottage consisting of a tiny sitting room, a bedroom and a bathroom. The walls had originally been light blue, Jacqueline guessed, but they had now taken on a general shade of dirty grey covered with smudges and fingerprints. The sheets on the beds were worn and old, but were freshly washed and clean. The bedroom boasted an air-conditioner, but she had no great expectations concerning its performance when she pushed the button. The machine gave a dark, deep grumble, then slowly laboured and sputtered into action, emitting a blast of cold air.

'It works!' she exclaimed.

'Enjoy it while it lasts,' Matt said cynically. 'It will probably break down, or the electricity will go off in the middle of the night.'

'And maybe it won't,' Jacqueline answered, refusing to let him dampen her enthusiasm.

When they had taken their suitcases out of the car,

Matt reached for his news magazine and collapsed on one of the beds. 'You go ahead first,' he said, pointing at the bathroom.

Jacqueline gathered her things and walked in. The bath was brown and rough from muddy water and old age. The shower stall held a large bucket of water and another bucket stood next to the toilet. She didn't have to try to know that the taps did not produce any water. It wasn't the first bucket bath she'd ever had, but it annoyed her that after a rotten day like this she couldn't even take a decent shower.

She stripped off her damp and dirty clothes and threw them on the floor, since there wasn't a chair or a stool to put them on. With the plastic cup from the bucket she splashed water all over her body and then lathered up from top to toe. With more cupfuls of clean water she rinsed off the soap and then dried herself off. Her hair, full of dust, needed a shampoo, but it would take too much water, so she left it and just brushed it as well as she could. She brushed her teeth, using water from the canteen, and then slipped on her cotton nightgown and robe. Already she felt sticky again, and not quite clean.

As she opened the door the cool air from the bedroom rushed at her and she sighed with relief. At least they might have a cool night's rest. Matt had fallen asleep and his magazine had dropped on his face. He looked strange lying there with his face hidden and Jacqueline smiled as she took off her robe and got into bed. She covered herself with the top sheet, pulling it up to her chin.

'Matt! Wake up! I'm finished!' He couldn't spend the night like that.

He groaned and sat up. The magazine fell to the floor.

'I don't know if it's worth it.'

'It is. You'll feel so much better when you're clean and you'll sleep better.'

'I suppose so.' He stood and looked at her in the bed. 'You don't want any dinner? Something exciting like rice and guinea-fowl stew?'

'No. All I want is sleep.'

Suddenly he grinned. 'Are you sure?'

'Yes!'

'This afternoon you told me you'd like to see a demonstration of how wonderful I am. This is your perfect opportunity.'

'Leave me alone!' She gripped the sheet as if it could possibly provide her with any kind of protection.

'Well, you'd better hold on to that sheet,' he said, the grin on his face widening. 'I may have some ideas of my own.'

Jacqueline felt like hitting him. Was he playing games with her? Did he think he was being amusing?

'You wouldn't dare!'

His eyebrows shot up. 'I wouldn't? Don't tempt me, little girl.' He picked up his things and disappeared in the bathroom.

Jacqueline closed her eyes, grateful for a temporary reprieve. He wasn't serious, she told herself. He wouldn't try anything. Matt wasn't that kind of a man. He just enjoyed playing games with her, making her feel uncomfortable. If all he wanted was to force her into something, he could have done so at home many times. He was making fun of her, that was all.

But she didn't feel half as secure as she wished she did and she waited nervously for him to come back to the room. He entered wearing nothing but a towel wrapped around his waist and Jacqueline's heart started racing at the sight of him. Tall, strong and deeply tanned, he looked like any woman's dream lover. She had the sudden terrible urge to go to him and touch him, put her cheek against his chest, move her fingers through his thick dark hair. . . .

'Will I do?' He gave her a lopsided grin and his eyes were full of amusement.

The blood rushed into her cheeks. 'You could have put something on!'

He shrugged. 'I never wear pyjamas. Who needs them in a climate like this? And I didn't bother bringing my robe. I'm sorry if I offended your sense of propriety, but I hadn't counted on these intimate sleeping arrangements.'

Jacqueline looked away. At all costs she wanted to prevent him seeing her confusion, but it was probably a useless effort. He knew her too well.

The mattress moved and she found Matt sitting at the edge of the bed, looking down on her with a smile.

'Are you scared?'

'Scared? Me? Why?' She tried to make her voice sound casual, but it was unmistakably thin and shaky.

'Don't pretend,' he said softly, and his tone of voice made her look up. Suddenly she saw a different man. The glow of amusement had left his face and there was tenderness in his eyes and something else she didn't understand. Something that made her heart flutter crazily and made her feel weak and shaky. Her eyes couldn't leave his face, and she had no idea how long they just looked at each other.

Gently he took her face between his hands. 'You're beautiful,' he said. 'You're beautiful in a very special way.' And then he bent down to kiss her. It was a warm and gentle kiss and it was the last thing she had expected. Her fear and resistance melted away with the warmth of his touch. Her heart pounded against her ribs with heavy, laboured beats. It was as if the world fell away and there was only the reality of this moment and the feeling of his lips on hers. She kissed him back with an urgency that both surprised and frightened her.

Feeling her response, his arms went around her back, lifting her up against him, holding her tightly. His kiss deepened with increasing passion, arousing in her needs and desires she couldn't control—didn't want to control. It was there again—the electricity, the sparks, the fire racing through her. Every nerve in her body tingled and the feeling of his hard, bare chest against her was sheer ecstasy.

Was this what she wanted? Was this what she had been waiting for? But she couldn't think, only kiss him, touch him. Nothing else mattered.

'Jackie,' he whispered. 'Oh, Jackie.' Then suddenly, abruptly, he released her and moved over to the other bed.

'Goodnight, Jackie.'

She was incapable of uttering a sound. Closing her eyes tightly, she huddled under the sheet, trembling. What had happened? Why had he left her just like that?

'Matt,' she whispered. 'Matt.' She didn't know what made her call out to him, or what she was going to say.

'Go to sleep, Jackie!'

She dared not say another word. Her mind was full of confusion and she couldn't calm down. Across the room she could hear his breathing. What was he thinking? What was he feeling? If only she knew! He wasn't sleeping, she was sure of that. There was a terrible, aching longing inside her, a longing for his touch, his lips, his hands. . . . It was madness, sheer madness. . . .

Exhaustion took over and eventually she fell asleep. When she awoke she heard Matt in the bathroom, whistling. He came back into the room, rubbing his face with a towel.

'Good morning, fair lady,' he said, throwing the towel on his bed. 'How did you sleep?' His voice was neutral, betraying nothing.

'Like a rock.'

He wore only pants and Jacqueline stared at his wide bare chest covered with dark curly hair, remembering the feel of it, remembering the way he'd held her and touched her. Impatient with herself, she shook her head, trying to clear her mind of the disturbing thoughts. It would be best to forget about it. And she knew, some-how, that Matt wasn't going to remind her of last night, either.

'What kind of day is it today?' she asked, as if one day could possibly be different from another.

He buttoned up his shirt and grinned. 'Let me make a guess. Sunny, hot, no precipitation. Temperature about ninety-five degrees if we're lucky. How does that sound?'

'Terrible!'

'How about getting out of bed? Or do you need help?'

'No, thanks. I'll be out as soon as you leave the room.' Her tone was light, as his had been.

'Okay, okay,' he grinned. 'I'm leaving. I'll be outside talking to the birds, but hurry, I'm starved. Oh, yes. Do take your things with you. We'll be back here tonight, but I don't like leaving the stuff sitting here all day.'

They were back on the road a little after seven. The world had already come alive and everywhere along the road women and girls were carrying large metal con-tainers of water on their heads. The air was very cool and the wind blowing through the open window chilled her. Jacqueline shivered.

'Are you cold?' Matt asked.

'Yes,' she said, winding up the window. 'It always

amazes me how fast the climate changes when you travel. One day north of Accra and the nights are colder already. You can feel the air is less humid, too.'

'Sahara Desert, here I come!'

Jacqueline smiled. The Sahara was still days of travel farther north. It presented the extremes in temperature—dry, blistering hot days, icy cold nights. She had a long-standing desire to see the desert, its people, its towns. She wanted to see camels and sand dunes and oases full of palms and orange trees. She had heard stories from friends who had hitch-hiked through the Sahara, from Ghana to Morocco.

It seemed like such a crazy, irresponsible thing to do, but apparently it had been quite possible. They had planned their route carefully and hadn't been particular about their physical comfort—how they travelled, where they slept and what they ate.

Jacqueline wasn't sure if her sense of adventure was quite up to that kind of travel, but she would love to see camels and mosques and visit cities like Bamako and Timbuctu. There was a ring of mystery and romance in those names. Her mind produced fleeting images of desert sheiks, veiled women and tall, haughty Tuaregs.

'What are you dreaming about?'

Jacqueline jerked upright and met Matt's eyes laughing into hers.

'Oh ... er ... would you believe Timbuctu?'

He shook his head and grinned. 'One day north of Accra and you're dreaming of the desert! Timbuctu, I'm afraid, isn't quite in the neighbourhood yet.'

'When I was a little girl I thought Timbuctu was some non-existent, magical place. Then I found out that it's a real town out in the desert, on the map and everything, and ever since, I've wanted to go there.'

He frowned. 'Well, let me see. If we forget about Mr

Minyila and his village, we can keep going and make it to Ougadougou today—easily, actually. Then we can go to the famous Hotel Indépendence and have a proper French dinner and a good night's sleep in luxury and comfort. Then tomorrow we can find out when there's a flight to Bamako. From there we take wonderful Air Mali and fly to Timbuctu. Presto!'

Jacqueline wrinkled her nose. 'Sounds much too easy and very unromantic.'

His eyebrows shot up. 'Oh, you want to do it the hard way? I forgot how tough you are. Well, how do you like the taste of sand and the smell of camels?'

She grinned. 'No idea. But Timbuctu sounds so terribly unreal and fascinating. It doesn't seem right to arrive there in a plane—much too prosaic.'

'Well, I've never been there, but friends have told me it's disappointing. There isn't much left of its historical and cultural glories. A couple of mosques, I believe. Now it's just another sandy desert town full of Arabs, Moors and Tuaregs.'

'Tuaregs! Your friends have no imagination!'

Matt bowed his head slightly. 'If you say so.'

Their talk had been light and easy and Jacqueline was relieved. She wasn't sure at all how to deal with last night's incident, or what to think about it. But Matt acted as if nothing had happened and his behaviour towards her was calm and friendly—nothing more. Yes, in a way she was relieved. They'd had enough strain and stress between them and she could do without more of that. But on the other hand she was confused by his behaviour. Somewhere in the back of her mind the thought of Diane disturbed her. She had left months ago and Matt never mentioned her. But Jacqueline wasn't at all sure that he didn't still love her and that she wouldn't come back one day. Her thoughts went around in circles.

Why did Matt hold her and kiss her as if he cared? Or was it only her imagination? It was true enough that his touch had the most profound effect on her, but that didn't mean she was doing the same to him.

I have to stop thinking about this, she thought angrily. It's not getting me anywhere. She shifted in her seat and looked outside. The scenery had changed considerably since they had left Accra the day before. The lush tropical green of the coastal region had disappeared and the land was yellow and dry. The huts were round rather than square and they stood huddled together in small clusters, presenting a cheerless picture—poor, dry and colourless.

A little while later they turned off the main road on to a rough, dusty track, barely wider than the car. It was several very slow and uncomfortable miles before they reached the village where Mr Minyila was waiting for them in the central square.

'I'm so glad you could come, Miss Donnelly,' he said with a strong American accent. He was wearing Muslim robes, but Kansas City obviously had left its mark. They followed him to his house, a multiple room structure of brown mud, where his younger brother served them coffee.

He's really magnificent, Jacqueline thought, looking at Mr Minyila. He was tall, handsome and very impressive in his white robe that stood out in sharp contrast to his black skin. She wondered if he had worn his robes in Kansas and when she asked him, his face glowed with amusement.

'Oh yes, in the summer, when it was hot. And of course to parties.' He grinned. 'It impressed the girls no end!'

I don't doubt it, Jacqueline thought, still amazed by the man's strange mixture of cultures: so American in speech and so African in looks.

Later they went back to the central square where the

whole village was waiting for them, including the chief, the elders and the local dance troupe.

The chief, an older version of Mr Minyila, tall, handsome and very regal, sat on a small leather pouffe on a platform covered with skins. The elders, also wearing long robes, sat on the steps of the platform. They were introduced to everyone and then they were seated—Matt on a wooden bench, Jacqueline in the only armchair available. Matt grinned at her and Jacqueline realised she was receiving special treatment. Had she not been present, Matt would have been offered the chair.

The chief made a long speech, translated by Mr Minyila, and while they were talking, Jacqueline took a careful look around her. They were sitting in the shade of the chief's house, a large compound consisting of several mud buildings including some that looked like warehouses for cotton. The village looked bare and dusty, with not a sign of green except a few nim and shea trees. The people stood around them in a circle and she noticed the children staring at her with large black eyes and serious faces.

It was Matt's turn for a speech and he began to explain the purposes of IFP and the way it operated. Again it was translated by Mr Minyila. Jacqueline watched Matt intently. She'd never seen him speak to such a large gathering and she couldn't help feeling a growing admiration for the way he handled himself. He was a good speaker, choosing his words with care and precision. It was obvious he held the people's attention. And her own. She liked looking at him. He stood tall and straight, his short-sleeved white shirt contrasting with his tanned face and arms, his thick hair glinting in the sun. He looked totally at ease with himself and the situation. Cutting across cultural and language barriers, he could even joke and make people laugh.

Matt's speech was followed by applause. Then the dance troupe appeared, accompanied by musicians carrying large drums. The dancers were young men dressed in shorts and wide blue and white shirts. The music was fast and frenzied and Jacqueline was fascinated by the wild grace of the dancers as they moved to the music. It went faster and faster until it made her dizzy just looking. Her head was filled with the rhythmic sounds of the drumming and the sun was beating down on her. She knew she was going to have a headache.

The formalities over, the villagers dispersed to go back to their daily duties of carrying water, pounding millet or baking pots. Matt and Jacqueline were left with the chief and the elders and they all sat down to serious business. Jacqueline took out her notebook and pen, ready to take notes.

'We have one thousand acres of land,' Mr Minyila began. 'We have cultivated cotton for many years now and as a result the soil is badly depleted. Cotton is not growing well any more and I've discussed with the elders and the people that I've been considering another crop—soy-beans.'

'What was their reaction?' Matt asked.

Mr Minyila frowned. 'Hesitant at first. They're not familiar with soy-beans. It's a new food for them. Later they decided it might be a good idea. After all, cotton can't be eaten at all and it is not giving us enough money any more.'

'You said the soil has been depleted. What will you do about that?'

The questions went on and on and Jacqueline scribbled away hastily. The heat of midday had descended upon them and she wiped the sweat off her face. Her hand was wet and stuck to the paper, which didn't make it easy to write. Fortunately her headache had not materialised, but she was thirsty and hungry.

Apparently she was not the only one. The discussion was over after half an hour and they were invited to the chief's compound for a meal. There was rice with guinea-fowl stew and beans with mutton stew. The food was very peppery and Jacqueline liked it. They had soft drinks and coffee and when the meal was over they went out to the fields to have a look at the land. The sun was scorching and the fields seemed to shimmer in the heat. They walked between the rows of scrawny-looking cotton plants, for hours it seemed. Jacqueline's feet ached and she was soaked with perspiration.

The cotton plants carried too few bolls and most of them were misformed. The soil was dry and cracked and ploughing and fertilising would be necessary before soybeans could be planted. She listened intently to Mr Minyila as he talked about his plans. But after an hour of this she heard nothing any more; it seemed that the sun had taken over and she needed all her energy to keep moving, to put one foot in front of the other.

The heat didn't seem to bother Matt quite as much. His shirt was soaked through, but he was still talking, asking questions, walking effortlessly over the parched ground.

It seemed hours later when they finally returned to Mr Minyila's house where they were given orange drinks that were cool, but not really cold.

'Can we see the clinic?' Jacqueline asked after she had somewhat recuperated.

'Yes, certainly!' Mr Minyila looked at his watch. 'It's after four, so Connie and Carol should be done for the day. Kurt isn't there. He went to Ouagadougou for a few days.' He smiled. 'He's the doctor, a German, and everybody here loves him. He's one fantastic guy. And the nurses ... they're wonderful. We're so lucky to have the three of them.'

The clinic was a simple white structure standing in the shade of a huge nim tree at the edge of the village. The two American nurses, Carol and Connie, greeted them warmly and proudly showed them around. They were a funny pair—one tall and thin, the other short and chubby. It was quite obvious that they were good friends, which was a blessing in their particular circumstances, Jacqueline thought.

'Can you stay for tea?' Connie, the chubby one, asked eagerly. She had a face full of freckles and large grey eyes that looked at them hopefully.

'We can't,' said Matt. 'We have to get back to Tamale. I don't like driving in the dark out here.'

'Oh, please!' Connie begged. 'We never get any visitors here.'

'Why don't you stay overnight?' Carol suggested. 'We have extra beds.' She stood calmly leaning against the wall, her hands in her uniform pockets. She was a much quieter person than Connie, but from the way she smiled, Jacqueline could tell that she was just as eager for their company as the other girl.

'Please?' Connie looked from Jacqueline to Matt. 'I'll tell you what! We have a big can of peaches from Ouagadougou. We'll open it and celebrate!'

Matt grinned. 'Oh, well, *peaches*! How can we resist?'

'Whoopee!' Connie yelled.

'Actually, it's not a bad idea,' said Matt. 'I have some questions about the people here that I'd like to ask you.'

The girls shared a small bungalow made of grey cement blocks that added no colour to the surroundings. They carried their luggage inside, and Jacqueline looked around with delight. Large, colourful posters hung on the

walls. There were shelves full of books and a stack of
games stood in a corner on the floor—Monopoly, Aggravation, Scrabble. There were some carved stools, a
large leather pouffe and some huge cushions covered
with market cloth. The room had a warm and cosy
atmosphere and Jacqueline felt instantly at home.

'Where does the doctor live?' she asked.

'In the house over there.' Carol pointed to an identical
bungalow on the other side of the path leading to the
clinic. 'Matt can stay there tonight. Kurt won't mind.
And Jacqueline can have the extra bed in my room.' Suddenly she coloured. 'If that arrangement suits you. I
mean ... you know, you can both stay at Kurt's place
if you prefer.'

Carol was obviously embarrassed and Jacqueline
laughed.

'No, thanks. I'm sure he snores.'

Matt looked at her, eyes narrowed. 'I don't snore! And
you know it.'

Now it was Jacqueline's turn to be embarrassed. The
two girls pretended to be busy. Carol left for the kitchen,
mumbling something about heating water for tea. Connie
cleared the coffee table and set out cups. Jacqueline
racked her brains for something suitable to say, but drew
a blank.

Matt grinned at her maliciously. 'You asked for it, you
got it.' He picked up his bags. 'I'll take these over right
now.' He turned to Connie. 'Is the door open, or do you
have a key?'

'It's open. We never lock up anything here. Stealing
from guests and visitors is taboo.'

When Matt had left, Connie looked at Jacqueline, her
eyes sparkling with laughter. 'Carol is such a prude. She
tries not to be, but she can't pull it off. You go right
ahead and stay there. Nobody is going to mind.'

Jacqueline shook her head. 'No, really. Matt was trying to embarrass me on purpose. He was referring to last night. We had to share a room at the Catering Resthouse because they fouled up the reservations.' She shrugged. 'I'm his Administrative Assistant. Strictly business, period.' Connie probably wouldn't believe her, but she didn't really care.

Connie giggled. 'Oh, my! Wait till Carol hears that! She'll be mortified.'

A minute later Carol entered the room with a tray and at the same time Matt came back inside.

'Don't you have a replacement for the doctor when he's gone?' he asked.

Carol shook her head. 'No, we manage on our own. If a case looks serious, we take the patient to the hospital in Tamale.'

'In our ambulance,' Connie said with a straight face.

'Oh, yes.' Matt's face was equally expressionless. 'That ancient heap of junk I saw outside.'

They drank tea and ate a plateful of homemade peanut butter cookies. Matt grinned at Jacqueline across the coffee table and she was sure he was still enjoying his little victory over her, but she smiled back at him, showing him that she didn't care. And she didn't. This was not the nineteenth century and the girls could think what they wanted. She poured herself another cup of tea.

'Don't you get lonely up here?' she asked. 'Not many people speak English, I imagine.'

'Sure we get lonely,' said Carol. 'But we all get along pretty well and that helps. Kurt is wonderful, and Baba comes here in the evenings sometimes.'

'Baba? Who's Baba?'

'Mr Minyila.' Connie laughed. 'He has the most incredible stories about his time in the States. He's real entertainment when he starts talking.'

'We know some people in Tamale, Dutch missionaries, and we get together sometimes,' Carol added. 'And we play a lot of games. Baba loves Monopoly.'

It turned out to be a very interesting evening. Jacqueline was filled with admiration for the nurses, their way of life, their patience, their stamina. Practising medicine the way they did, with few supplies and makeshift measures, was any doctor's nightmare.

'How do you stay sane?' Jacqueline asked, half joking, half serious.

Connie pulled a face and looked cross-eyed. 'I don't. Can't you tell?'

Carol smiled and looked at her friend. 'She's ready for a vacation. She's going to Accra next month.'

'Vacation, hah!' Connie said indignantly. 'I'm going to pick up some medical supplies at the harbour and I have to talk to some people at the Peace Corps office. Some fun that's going to be!'

The next morning they left the village laden with gifts—ten pounds of brown rice, two guinea-fowl squawking in the back of the car, and three dozen tiny guinea-fowl eggs.

'I hate to take this food,' Jacqueline said to Matt. 'Talk about taking food out of babies' mouths!'

Matt shrugged. 'There's no alternative unless we want to insult them terribly by refusing it.'

They finally managed to leave, with every man, woman and child waving them out.

'See you in Accra!' Connie yelled at the top of her voice.

'One thing I know I could never do,' said Jacqueline, 'is to be a nurse out in the bush with no place to go and only a handful of kindred souls to talk to. I'd go stark raving mad!'

'You like your parties and your dinners, don't you?'

'It's not the parties or dinners as such,' she said angrily. 'I need people around me! I enjoy being with different kinds of people, finding out what they've done and where they've been.'

'My comment wasn't meant as criticism, Jackie. Just a statement.' He smiled and shook his head. 'We're always too touchy with each other, you know that? We should try to relax a little.'

We he had said, not *you*. Did he mean that he was touchy with her too? Well, it was true, wasn't it? They often irritated each other. Seemingly little things could make the sparks of their hostility fly. But this had been a nice trip. She'd enjoyed it and they'd been constantly in each other's company—even at night in Tamale. A warm glow filled her, thinking of that night in the rest-house, remembering his kisses, his arms around her. You'd better forget it, she told herself for the umpteenth time. She looked outside, forcing her mind clear of thoughts of Matt.

They drove to Kumasi and stayed overnight in the City Hotel. The next day Matt had business in the morning and Jacqueline roamed through the city for a couple of hours. They drove back to Accra in the afternoon.

For the next few days there was nothing but work, work, work. Jacqueline wrote a report about their trip to the north, putting a great deal of effort into it. She wanted it to be good. She wanted to prove she could do it. It was terribly important that she should not disappoint Matt. So far he'd been satisfied with her work, acknowledging on more than one occasion that he found her competent and efficient.

Still, she wasn't satisfied, she didn't quite know why. She was hungry for his approval, but the faint, restless stirrings she felt sometimes made her wonder if there was something else she wanted. Something more than just professional appreciation for her work.

Thoughts about the night in Tamale often came to her at unexpected moments. The memories seemed to linger on and on, making her feel uneasy with herself. So many times Matt had aggravated her, irritated her, infuriated her, but when he had held her and kissed her he had been a different man—warm and loving and tender. He had evoked in her emotions she was not yet prepared to evaluate. He hadn't kissed her just for the fun of it; she couldn't believe that. But if he had kissed her because he liked her and enjoyed the intimacy, why then had he withdrawn from her so abruptly? Was Diane still with him in his thoughts? Was he still in love with her? And if so, did it matter?

Yes, it did. It was humiliating to know that at his every touch she felt herself go limp, giving in to him without resistance. She didn't want him to have that kind of power over her—not if all he really wanted was Diane.

One morning while she was working she found Matt standing in her office door.

'Jackie?'

Switching off her calculator, she looked up. 'Yes?'

'Are you very busy? I'd like to talk to you. It's important.'

'I'll be finished with this in a minute. I'll be right over.'

'Fine.' He strode back into the reception area and she heard him order two coffees. 'And I don't want to be disturbed,' he told Patience.

Something important. But what? She couldn't imagine what it could be. Not on the business level anyway. Nothing earth-shaking had happened or was expected to happen. And on the personal level everything between them was calm and quiet. Suddenly a shattering thought entered her mind.

Diane was coming back. That was it. That had to be it! Matt had been in a good mood all morning. He was going to tell her that Diane was coming back, that they were getting married, that she would have to leave the flat and find herself another place to live.

Jacqueline didn't like it. Not one bit. The flat had become her home; she didn't want to leave now. And she didn't want Diane to come back.... Her mind was in turmoil and she felt suddenly sick.

CHAPTER SIX

HE was sitting at his desk when she entered his office. Two cups of coffee were waiting and she helped herself to one and sat down. She was aware of his eyes studying her.

'What's the matter with you?' he asked.

'Nothing. I mean, I was wondering what the important news was.'

'Cheer up. It's good news.'

'For you, or for me?'

'For both of us.'

'Oh.' It was not a very intelligent reply, but it was all she was capable of at the time.

'What were you thinking of?'

She shrugged. 'I don't know. I just wondered if it was bad. Maybe something I'd done wrong. Something ... I don't know.' Her words were as confused as her thoughts and she shook her head, trying to clear her mind. 'Never mind. Tell me the great news.'

He folded his arms and tipped his chair back. 'How would you like a raise?'

'A raise? Me!' It was the last thing she had expected.

'You.' He grinned. 'Don't get your hopes up too high. It won't be much. Just *small small*.'

Jacqueline swallowed. A raise. She liked it, of course, but was it such important news? After what she had been thinking, she was more relieved than happy.

'Why is that good news for you?' she asked.

'Because you're going to have to do something for it. I want you to take over the initial project screenings. Remember the report you wrote on Mr Minyila's village?'

'Yes, of coure.'

'It was excellent. Your writing is very good. You showed a clear insight into the problems of that particular situation; it was noticeable in the way you put together the report.' He leaned forward, looking at her closely. 'It made me feel confident about your judgments. From now on I want you to deal with all incoming project requests. Answer the mail and handle the interviews with the people coming in for information.' He stirred his coffee and smiled. 'You look slightly overwhelmed.'

'I am. I'm not trained in project development.'

'The initial stages aren't very complicated and you've had enough exposure. And, as I said, I trust your judgment.'

'I'm ... I'm very pleased. Tell me what I should do.'

'The first screening is simple. You get letters from people telling you they want money to buy a tractor to cultivate their two-acre plot of maize. No good. You write them a polite letter saying sorry, we don't give away money, only technical and managerial assistance. Maybe you get a letter requesting assistance setting up a sugar factory. Sugar factories are very popular these days, but they don't meet our criteria. Sugar is not quality food. It provides empty calories and doesn't promote health.' He waved his hand. 'Out it goes.'

He leafed through a folder, took out a letter. 'Here's your test. A Mr Donker requesting assistance with the cultivation of cashew nuts. He has excellent qualifications, land, some money. What do you think?'

Jacqueline thought about it for a moment, then shook her head. 'No good.'

'No?' He looked surprised. 'Cashews are a source of protein.'

'More likely a source of foreign exchange. They

wouldn't be used for local consumption. They'd go straight for export and end up at London cocktail parties.'

He grinned. 'Good thinking! I thought I might trip you up with that one.' He leafed through the folder again. 'Anyway, there are several promising ones—cow-peas, soy-beans, instant weaning food for babies. Have a look and see what you think.'

'What do I do with the ones I don't reject?'

'That's step two. Do some research on the subject. Find out what's been tried before, and how.' He gave her some more details and Jacqueline could feel herself grow restless with excitement. Shifting her position, she crossed her arms and hugged herself.

'It sounds terribly interesting. I've wanted to get more involved with the actual project work.'

He studied her face for a long moment, his eyes full of warmth and something else she didn't know how to interpret. She'd seen that look before, that night in Tamale. The memories came rushing at her with alarming clarity. Emotions overwhelmed her, frightening her with their intensity. She felt a sudden wild desire to feel his lips on hers again, his arms around her, his body close to hers. Looking at his face, she had the crazy notion he was thinking the same thing. Her heart lurched. For one timeless moment his gaze held hers, then he looked down again at the papers on his desk.

'Step three is this.' He continued talking, his voice calm and unperturbed. Pulling herself together, Jacqueline concentrated once more on what he was saying.

Walking back to her own office a while later, she felt happy and excited. Her new assignment had proven that Matt had confidence in her and trusted her with more responsibility. It was important to her that he did, she didn't deny it. But there had been more. She had sensed it in that elusive moment he had looked at her with that strange expression in his eyes. Something more than just professional appreciation—something deeper, something. . . .

Jacqueline sat down at her desk, her face in her hands. Don't do this to yourself, she thought. Don't make something out of nothing. Don't imagine something that wasn't there. . . .

Pushing all other thoughts aside, she began to concentrate on her work. Late in the afternoon her phone rang.

'Howdy, howdy! Long time no see.'

'David!' she exclaimed.

He'd been in Washington for two weeks and she hadn't seen him since before her trip to the north.

'How about dinner tonight?'

'I'd love to, but I'm treating. I just got a raise today.'

'How about that! So much for the little schoolgirl not being taken seriously.'

Jacqueline laughed. 'I've lots to tell you.'

They had a nice, leisurely meal at the Palm Court. Afterwards they went for a walk on the beach, their shoes in their hands, talking and laughing. The wet sand was cool on her bare feet.

After a while they fell silent and just walked and listened to the sounds of the sea. The beach was still and deserted. Jacqueline loved the solitude, the absence of crowds and heat and noise that was so much a part of life in Accra.

'Let's sit down,' said David, dropping down in the sand. He pulled her beside him.

A light breeze stroked her face. David's hand came up and brushed a curl behind her ear. 'Your hair is coming loose. Why don't you let it down?'

There was an odd tone in his voice and suddenly she felt a strange sensation she couldn't define.

'David. . . .'

'Don't talk.' His arms went around her and he gently pushed her back on the sand. His mouth covered hers and she could feel his rising passion as he kissed her, Apprehension mounted in her. He had never kissed her like this before. She turned her face away. 'No, David, please. . . .'

His mouth was next to her ear. 'I want you, Jackie.'

Her body stiffened in his arms. 'No, David. Please!'

'What's the matter?'

'I can't. I just can't.' She moved out of his arms, away from him, feeling miserable and close to tears. She didn't want this. She hadn't asked for it.

'Hey, Jackie, come here.' His voice was low and controlled. 'There's nothing to be scared about. I'm not the raping kind.'

She covered her face with her hands. 'David, I'm so sorry. I don't want you to be serious about me. I don't want to disappoint you. I. . . .'

'You don't love me.' It was a statement, not a question.

'Not in that way. I. . . .'

'Come here, Jackie.' He took her hand. 'Let's talk about this.'

She moved closer and he put his arm lightly around her shoulder.

'Okay. Point one: You're my friend, Jackie. I like being with you. We have fun together and good talks. You feel, you think—you're a real person. Point two: Besides being a real person, you're also a real woman.' He paused and looked at her. 'And I happen to be an ordinary guy. It wouldn't be very normal if I didn't want to sleep with you.'

'I suppose not.'

'You bet your life not!'

'You must think I'm not normal.'

He laughed. 'Let's say inexperienced. Or unawakened.'

Colour surged into her face and she bit her lip. 'Is it that obvious?'

He nodded, smiling at her. There was amusement in his eyes and she felt like a silly little girl.

'Are you making fun of me?'

'Small-small.' He pulled her up. 'Don't worry about it. And don't make a big deal of it. One day your fires will go roaring and you'll know.' He picked up his shoes and shook the sand out. 'In the meantime, if you don't mind, I'll stick around and enjoy your most excellent companionship. And I'll try to keep my own fires under control.'

She laughed with a great sense of relief. 'You're a real friend, David.'

'Sure. Let me know when you're ready for a lover.'

'Oh, David! Don't make me feel bad.'

He wasn't trying to make her feel bad, she knew. But still she couldn't help feeling guilty. Not for having refused him, but because she didn't feel more for him than a warm friendship, as if somehow she could dictate her own feelings and emotions.

Silently they plodded through the sand back to the car. Did David love her? He had never mentioned it and she had assumed he felt the same towards her as she did to him. Why couldn't it just be easy and simple?

'Listen, Jackie, I can hear your mind grinding this thing over, making a big thing out of nothing.' He dropped his shoes and put his hands on her shoulders. 'Look at me. I know you don't love me. I wasn't asking for love, you know that. And I'm sorry about what happened. I should have known that for you nothing but the real thing will do.'

No words would come and she kept silent.

'Now forget it, Jackie. Please.'

She nodded numbly, looking up into his eyes, seeing him smile.

'Okay then.' He picked up his shoes again. 'I'll race you to the car!'

Matt was not home when she returned. His car was gone and he was probably at the Tesano Sports Club where he spent much of his free time swimming and playing tennis.

She went inside and got ready for bed, shaking out her clothes and brushing her hair. There was sand everywhere and it stuck to her skin. Only a shower would get rid of it.

She couldn't sleep. Her mind was going around in circles, thinking about David, about Matt. Why couldn't she just love David? He was nice. He was a real friend. But he didn't stir her deeper feelings. And Matt? His kisses had aroused her; she didn't deny it. Pure physical attraction? The right chemistry at work? Or were her feelings more involved? Was it love?

She turned over, pressing her face into the pillow. Her head was splitting and her eyes ached. Love? What was love? Would she ever recognise it?

So many people made mistakes. There were so many bad relationships, unhappy marriages, divorces. Matt and Diane—something was wrong there too. He was bitter and disappointed, and when Jacqueline had arrived he'd taken it out on her. She understood that better now. And now Matt spent his free time playing sports and showed no interest in women. At least she'd never noticed anything of the sort. Did he love Diane? Was he still waiting for her to change her mind and come back? But after all those months, surely it was a hopeless situation.

Her headache was not getting any better and she got

out of bed to look for some aspirin. But she couldn't find any and she couldn't remember what she'd done with the bottle the last time she'd used it. Maybe there was some in Matt's bathroom. She didn't like the idea of snooping around in his private quarters, but she needed something for her throbbing head or she wouldn't sleep all night.

But there was no aspirin in his medicine cabinet, either, and she didn't see it anywhere else in the bathroom. This was ridiculous! Why couldn't she find some of those blasted tablets! As she walked back into the hallway, she heard the front door open and she entered the living room the same time Matt did. He was dressed in white shorts and shirt and was carrying a tennis racquet.

Jacqueline felt acutely embarrassed, as though he had caught her in some indecent or improper act.

'I ... I was looking for some aspirin. I didn't have any.' Her hair fell in front of her eyes and she nervously pushed it back. 'I looked in your bathroom, but there's none there. I hope you don't mind.' She looked at him uncomfortably.

Matt only grinned. 'I don't keep any great big secrets in my bathroom. And the aspirin, I believe, is in the kitchen. I had some yesterday and I think I left it there. Sit down, I'll get it.'

She heard him open the refrigerator and pour some water in a glass. He came back in the room and handed her two tablets and the glass. 'Headache?'

She nodded. 'Yes.' She swallowed the aspirins down with the water. She couldn't keep her eyes off him; he looked so good in his tennis outfit. His legs were straight and strong, and his tan stood out against the white of his clothes. His hair looked tousled and she felt the crazy urge to move her fingers through the thickness of it. His eyes caught hers.

'Are you all right otherwise?' His hand touched her

forehead and suddenly she shivered. He frowned. 'You're taking anti-malarial medicine, aren't you?'

'Yes. Yes, of course.'

'What kind? Chloroquine? Paludrine?'

'Chloroquine.'

'Well, I don't think you have a fever.'

'I just have a headache, that's all.' His concern made her uncomfortable.

He gave her a lopsided smile. 'I was just making sure. Can't afford to have my AA get sick, you know.'

For some reason, his comment irritated her. If she was going to be sick, she was going to be sick whether he liked it or not. She wasn't indispensable. The office could run itself for a couple of days, if that was what worried him. She rose to her feet, pulling her robe closer around her. She shook her hair behind her shoulders. 'I'd better go to bed now. Thanks for the aspirin.'

Her headache was gone the next morning and she felt good. Entering the living room for breakfast, she found Matt already there. He looked up from his paper.

'Good morning. How's the headache?'

'It's all gone, thanks.'

Jacqueline went to the kitchen to get some coffee, greeting Kwesi who was making scrambled eggs and toast. It was a cloudy morning and it looked like rain.

'It's dark in here,' she remarked, flipping on the light switch.

'It's trying to rain,' Kwesi said, looking gloomy. He didn't like rain.

The morning went by quickly. The monthly financial reports were finished in record time. The system she had developed worked very well.

After lunch she was reading a report on the goat farming project when suddenly a gust of wind blew through the open windows and scattered her papers all over the floor. Somewhere in the building a door slammed, then another. She closed the windows and stood still for a moment, watching the paw-paw trees and the coconut palms swaying in the wind. It was more like a storm, getting stronger every second. It was so dark now she had to turn on the light. Soon the sky would burst open and sheets of rain would come lashing down. The change of weather was welcome. Jacqueline liked the rain, the smells of wet earth, the sounds of dripping foliage.

Having gathered her papers off the floor, she sat down again and sorted them out. There was a knock on the door and Patience entered with a cup of coffee. The cup was rattling on its saucer and Jacqueline noticed that the girl looked shaken.

'Are you afraid of the rain, Patience?'

'No, oh, no. . . . There's something wrong with Mr Simmons. She put the cup on the desk and hugged herself, shivering.

'Something wrong? What do you mean?'

'I brought his mail a few minutes ago, and he was fine then. He asked me to get him some coffee and when I came back with it, he . . . he looked so . . . so strange. He didn't even see me when I gave him his cup.' Her eyes were wide and worried as she looked at Jacqueline. 'It was not good, Miss Donnelly.'

Jacqueline was out of the door before she knew what she was doing. She gave a short rap on Matt's half open door and entered. He didn't look up and a sudden frightening premonition stopped her as she stared at the strangely hunched figure in the chair. It wasn't like Matt to hang in a chair like a deflated balloon.

Her legs felt like rubber as she came a few steps closer. 'Matt, is something wrong?'

He sat staring at some papers in front of him. Slowly he looked up. His face was grey and his eyes were filled with a dark, unreadable emotion.

'Wrong? No, nothing's wrong any more.' He gave a short, joyless laugh. 'Nothing's wrong. Everything is straightened out and cleared up.'

Jacqueline winced at the bitterness in his voice and she watched him as he gathered the papers and stuffed them in his briefcase. With a violent jerk he shoved his chair back and stood up.

'Excuse me, please.' He moved past her, out of the door.

Something was terribly wrong. She stood very still, not knowing what to do. The front door slammed back on its spring. A car started and she heard it crunch down the gravelled driveway.

The next moment the rain came pelting down, sending shivers down her spine. A sense of dread and apprehension filled her. She had no idea what Matt had been talking about, or where he was going now.

Back in her office she found her coffee, lukewarm and sweetened. She'd given up sugar long ago, and it tasted terrible. Patience came back into her office, a fearful expression on her face.

'Is he all right?' she asked.

'I don't know, Patience. He went home, I think.' At least she hoped that was where he'd gone in this weather. She sighed. 'I'd like some more coffee. No sugar, please.'

'Oh, I put sugar in your coffee! Oh, I'm so sorry!' The girl looked totally flustered, guilty to the core.

Jacqueline sighed again, feeling tired and weary. 'Patience, it doesn't matter. It's not important. You were thinking of other things.'

'Yes, madame.' She took the cup and hurried out of the room.

Jacqueline wished Patience wouldn't act as if she were charged with a mortal crime whenever someone pointed out a slip or error. Patience worked so well and tried so hard, there was no reason for her to be so insecure.

The rain continued coming down and the dark wetness of the world seemed gloomy now, and depressing. Jacqueline felt jittery and nervous and got nothing more accomplished for the rest of the afternoon.

At five o'clock, the rain still hadn't stopped and Jacqueline drove Patience and Samson home so they wouldn't have to stand in the rain waiting for a bus.

The house was deserted when she returned. Matt was not home, and it was Kwesi's night off. Where was Matt? Where could he be in this weather? Well, why should she worry about him? He could take care of himself perfectly well.

She made a meal of leftovers, but at seven he was still gone and she wondered if she should eat or wait for him a while longer. The rain was coming down in a steady stream and the house was dark and gloomy. An increasing sense of foreboding took hold of her. Maybe something had happened to him. A car accident. Something. Maybe she should call someone, but whom? David?

When David answered the phone, she let out a sigh of relief.

'Oh, I'm so glad you're home!' she exclaimed.

'Why? Something wrong?'

'It's Matt. He's gone. I don't know where he is.' She told him what had happened, but David only laughed.

'Jacqueline, you sound like a worried wife! For Pete's sake, he's a grown man. He can take care of himself. Relax.'

'I ... I tried. But I can't help feeling strange about it, David. I don't know why. He looked so terrible!'

It was quiet for a long time.

'Okay, Jackie, I'll check around.'

'Oh, David, thank you!'

'Sure.'

The food was tasteless and she put it in a bowl to give to Ali's dog. She went to the garage and found Ali sitting on a low stool, talking to his friend, the watchman from the house across the street. They were eating rice and stew from little blue enamel pans. Ali took the food for the dog and thanked her.

'Massa, he no come?' he asked.

'No, Mr Simmons is not home. He'll come later.'

The hours dragged by. Finally the rain stopped and the sausage flies came out by the thousands. Strange insects, looking like winged caterpillars. They flew up against the windows, beating crazily against the screens, trying to get in. Many of them succeeded, but how they managed it with all the doors closed and the windows screened was a mystery. They flew drunkenly around the lightbulbs, crashing on furniture and floors, losing their silky, transparent wings. It was all part of their primitive ritual and Jacqueline watched the wingless creatures as they crawled away. Tomorrow they would be gone and Kwesi would go through the house, sweeping up the silky wings scattered round everywhere.

Outside, in the gutters and the grass, the frogs had come out too, thousands of them it seemed, croaking hoarsely and continuously, making her nerves stand on end.

Where was Matt?

The rain had cooled the air and she shivered in her cotton dress. Having cleared her bath tub of half a dozen sausage flies, she took a warm shower and dressed in jeans and a T-shirt. She didn't want to go to bed. She wouldn't sleep.

It was after eleven when the phone rang.

'Were you in bed?' David asked.

'No.' Her voice shook.

'I didn't think so. Jackie, he's on his way home. He should be there any moment now.'

Relief washed over her. 'Where was he?'

'I'm not sure where he was this afternoon, but he came here just after you called. Jackie ... he's had a few drinks. He was here all evening, talking. I couldn't call you with him sitting right here.'

'No, of course not. I understand. Is ... is he terribly drunk?'

David laughed. 'No, no, just *small-small*. But I did insist on Kofi driving him home. Kofi can take a taxi back here.'

'Kofi? Oh, yes, your steward. I'm sorry, I'm such a scatterbrain tonight.'

'Well, the lost sheep is found, so you can sleep tonight.'

The gate squeaked and then car tires crunched the gravel. 'He's here, David. I hear the car. I'd better hang up.'

'Call me if you need me, okay?'

'Yes, I will. Thanks so much, David.'

Her heart was pounding as she watched Matt come through the door. His face looked grey and drawn, his eyes dark and unreadable.

'Little girls should be in bed at this hour,' he drawled.

'Couldn't sleep. Those blasted frogs make too much noise.' She tried to sound casual.

He collapsed on the sofa. 'Come sit here, Jackie.' He patted the seat next to him. 'I want to talk. We never talk. All we ever do is fight.'

Not any more, she thought. We haven't fought for weeks.

'I was on my way to the kitchen to make some coffee,' she said carefully. 'Would you like a cup?'

He looked at her wearily. 'Jackie, I know I've been drinking, but I'm not roaring drunk. But yes, please, I'd like some coffee.'

The cups rattled in her hands. She dropped a spoon. This is crazy, she thought. I'm shaking like a leaf. The coffee jar was almost empty. I'll have to go to Lomé again soon, she thought stupidly.

'David is a first class guy,' Matt said as he took the cup from her. 'You're a lucky girl, Jackie.'

She bit her lip. 'David is a good friend. I've known him for a long time.'

'It's good to know somebody for a long time,' he said obscurely.

She wasn't sure what to say or do, and she just sat there, next to him, drinking her coffee. Occupied by his own thoughts, Matt stared into his cup, and for a while it was very quiet except for the incessant croaking of the bullfrogs outside.

Jacqueline clenched her fingers around her cup in helpless frustration. If only she knew what to say, if only she knew how to reach out to him, help him, do something. But she didn't even have any idea what had happened to him.

Suddenly he put down his cup and rose to his feet. 'I want to show you something. Come along.' He took her hand and pulled her out of the room, into his bedroom. She'd never been there before. It was large and had a wooden floor like the rest of the house. At the far end was a big bed covered with a brightly coloured Kente cloth that must have cost a fortune. Matt went to the dresser and took something out of the drawer and gave it to her.

'Who do you think this is?'

It was a picture of a girl in a black string bikini standing on a beach with coconut palms in the background. She was beautiful—very tall, with long, slender limbs and masses of red hair hanging down her shoulders in heavy curls. Jacqueline's throat felt dry and she swallowed.

'It's your ...' She hesitated. 'Your fiancée.'

His laugh was short and bitter. '*Fiancée*. Yes, that's what I thought. That's what everybody thought.'

'I don't know what you mean,' she said, her voice sounding strange and low in her own ears.

'She never intended to marry me, you know. She never did.' He laughed again, a cold and joyless sound. She wished he would stop it. His laughing hurt her deep inside.

Matt walked to the bed and dropped himself on it, kicking off his shoes. 'She never did intend to marry me,' he repeated, staring up at the ceiling with empty eyes.

CHAPTER SEVEN

THE picture burned in Jacqueline's hand. She stared at it a moment longer, then put it down on the dresser, searching her mind for something to say. Lying on the bed, Matt was watching her.

'Come here, Jackie. Don't just stand there.'

Her legs wouldn't move and she couldn't bear to look at him. He seemed a stranger now, in the grip of some terrible emotion she didn't understand. Was it anger, sorrow, bitterness? A combination of all? She wasn't sure.

'Sit down, Jackie.' He patted the bed. 'Don't worry, I don't get violent when I drink.'

Obviously he had noticed her hesitation. She sat down on the edge of the bed, feeling cold and shivering a little. Outside the chorus of frogs went on and on. Where did they all come from? she wondered vaguely. And what am I doing here in this room? she thought, apprehension rising in her.

'Diane was a model. Did you know that?'

'Yes.' Her voice was barely a whisper. She didn't want to talk about Diane, listen to his confidences. But he seemed unaware of her unease.

'She was beautiful and quite successful. I met her in Kenya. Ever been there?'

'No.' She wished he would stop. She wanted to get up and leave, but some strange and inexplicable force held her there, as if she were tied to the bed.

'She was on assignment there, doing a series on the new summer fashions. They like to do that in exotic places—elephants and lions lurking in the background,

133

some dirty little kids with barely a stitch on scattered around for effect. God, how obscene can you get, standing there in your five-hundred-dollar dress in the middle of a bunch of kids who hardly have enough to eat!' He stared up at the ceiling.

Jacqueline said nothing. There wasn't anything to say. Nervously she fingered the handwoven material of the bedspread, her eyes caught by the brilliance of the colours. Orange, blue, green....

'Of course, I didn't see that then,' he continued. 'All I saw was her. I fell in love with all that red hair.' He laughed bitterly. 'And she fell in love with my Land Rover. She had some crazy notions about my life-style. Thought I was some glamorous white hunter type.'

It was easy enough to see. He looked like a white hunter with his strong, tanned body, his rugged, square-jawed face and his dark eyes that reflected a touch of arrogance and superiority. Put him in a safari suit in a Land Rover and the picture was complete. But Jacqueline knew about his job in Kenya—it had involved a lot of hard work, dust and sweat. And very little glamour.

'Well, it wasn't so bad in the beginning. Nairobi is quite a sophisticated city. There's a lot to do and at least she wasn't bored. Then she came here. Can you imagine a girl like Diane in a place like this? Can't even buy a decent lipstick. She hated it here. And she hated me for not living up to her expectations. She belonged in New York, with the jet set. There was nothing for her here.' He shook his head. He hadn't looked at Jacqueline while he talked and she wondered if he had forgotten she was there.

Suddenly he laughed coldly. 'And I wanted to marry her—a girl like that. How stupid could I be! She didn't believe in marriage, she said. One of those liberated types—no strings, no commitments. She laughed at me, saying I was too old-fashioned, that I took life much too seriously. But like a fool I kept hoping she'd change her mind.' His voice was full of self-contempt. He turned his gaze towards Jacqueline. 'What about you, Jackie? Would you want to marry me?'

Her heart pounded painfully against her ribs. 'Matt, I....'

'You've got a lot more going for you than Diane. You like this place and you're not scared of every creepy-crawly. You eat the food and you don't cry about short-ages or complain about servants and heat and boredom.' His lips curled into a lopsided smile. 'You even have your own secret super-duper witches' handbook to tell you how to make dishwash soap. And you care about your work.' His eyes went back to the ceiling. 'Diane ... she didn't give a damn about my work. Used to laugh at me. "Matthew the World-Saver," she called me.'

Jacqueline's eyes were drawn to his face, taking in the deep lines next to his mouth, the bitter twist of his lips. There was a deep, aching sadness inside her and she looked away, surveying the room, not really seeing any-thing. He was silent for a long time and when she stole a look at him again, his eyes were closed. She thought he was asleep, but when she tried to stand up he grabbed her arm and pulled her down beside him.

'Don't go, Jackie. Please stay with me.' He muttered the words, half asleep, as he put his arms around her, holding her close to him.

Her head was spinning and the blood pounded in her ears so loudly, it almost drowned out the vibrating sounds of the croaking frogs. She was acutely aware of his body so close to hers on the big bed. His face was turned towards her, relaxed in sleep, A sudden, over-whelming urge took hold of her. She wanted to put her face against his, stay in his arms for the rest of the night.

Her feelings alarmed her and she moved her eyes away from him.

I'm crazy, she thought. I must be out of my mind.

Later, when he moved into deeper sleep, his arms relaxed and fell away from her body. As quietly as possible she slipped off the bed and went back to her own room.

The morning was bright and clean and very hot. Matt arrived at the breakfast table looking his usual self.

'I must apologise for last night,' he said, looking straight at her. 'I'm not in the habit of getting drunk.'

'I know.'

His eyes studied her for a moment. 'Yes, I suppose you do.'

He ate his eggs, apparently not suffering from any after-effects of his drinking. 'I'm sorry if I was obnoxious,' he said.

'You weren't obnoxious and you weren't all that drunk, either. Just a little under the weather,' Jacqueline said lightly.

'I'm not sure just what I told you last night, but I might as well give you the facts straight and with a sober mind.'

Jacqueline bit her lip and stared at her plate. 'No, please don't. You owe me no explanations. Just forget it.'

He must have sensed her discomfort, because a ghost of a smile slipped around his lips while he observed her.

'It was that bad?'

She flushed. 'No. I t wasn't bad at all, just....'

'Just what?'

She thought for a moment, not knowing how to explain her feelings to him. Maybe the straight facts were the best and the simplest.

'You wanted me to stay and listen to you. You were telling me things that were none of my business, but I couldn't stop you. You wanted to talk.'

'I see.' He drank his coffee. 'Well, to keep things short and simple, Diane and I met in Kenya, not long before I came over here. I wanted to marry her, but she had other inclinations. She was here with me for a while, but didn't like it. Then she left. Yesterday I got a letter from her stating that she wasn't coming back and that she considered our relationship terminated. She repeated a few of her opinions about me and my life-style that I find objectionable, if not insulting. So I got drunk, for which I again apologise. The whole thing was not really a surprise, so why I got boozed up, God only knows. It was a stupid thing to do. She wasn't worth it.' His voice was cool and calm and he spoke as if he were ordering a steak and salad.

Jacqueline stared at him in numb silence, her mind a whirlpool of confusing thoughts.

Matt took one last gulp from his coffee and rose to his feet. 'And now let's get to work.'

Another week came and went with more rain and more dampness. One of Matt's wood carvings turned green with mildew and so did a pair of Jacqueline's sandals she did not wear often. Kwesi had trouble getting the laundry dry and spent much time carrying clothes back and forth to the line.

Matt had not referred again to the night he had confided in her, but Jacqueline wasn't able to banish from her mind the things he had told her.

Matthew the World-Saver, Diane had called him. The words were devastatingly cruel. Jacqueline had worked with Matt long enough to know he had no such pretensions. He didn't work for money or fame or out of some misguided notion that he was God's answer to Africa. His idealism didn't get in the way of his common sense or the reality of the business world. But deep down inside him there were the convictions of every man's equality and his right to a decent existence. Diane had taken his beliefs and twisted them cruelly, mocked them with those brutal words. What had made her do that? A desire to hurt? Jealousy? Disappointment? He had not lived up to her expectations. Obviously she hadn't known him well enough to realise that he was a man with strong feelings about his work and his life. She hadn't been able to share those feelings, only ridicule them. Her life as a model hadn't prepared her for the kind of existence Matt had to offer.

Reading in her room at night, Jacqueline had trouble concentrating on her book. Her mind kept wandering off, always coming back to the same subject, the same question.

Had he really loved Diane?

Of course he had loved her! For a fleeting moment she had a strong feeling of resentment, a sharp pang of jealousy. Did Matt still love her? She hadn't wanted to ask herself that question, but it had been in the back of her mind for a long time. Did he still love her, despite the differences, despite the fact that she had treated him badly? It hadn't left him undisturbed when he had received that letter from her. In fact, he had disappeared for hours and then returned shaken, shocked and confused. He had talked too much and with a lot of bitterness. He had not expressed himself in glorifying terms about Diane, but if he didn't love her any more, why then had he seemed so totally devastated?

She wished she knew.

Jacqueline's birthday was the first of August and as the day drew closer she felt more and more depressed. She'd never mentioned it to anyone. She couldn't very well tell

David it was her birthday and ask him to please take her out to dinner, and then have him feel obliged to buy her some present as well.

I'm acting like a child, she thought irritably. I'm turning twenty-four, not four. Who needs a cake with candles?

The day arrived and nothing happened. She felt utterly lonely, forsaken, forgotten. Not even a card from her parents. Well, maybe tomorrow. There was always tomorrow. But her depression didn't go away and not even Steven with his boisterous laugh and his crazy goat jokes could pull her out of her self-pity.

It was almost five and she was ready to go home when a memo from Matt was brought in by Patience.

Any plans for tonight? the memo read. Jacqueline stared at the large round letters sprawled across the paper. Did Matt know it was her birthday? Why hadn't he mentioned it before? She shrugged. More likely he wanted to find out if she could spend some extra time at the office, or work on a special project at home tonight, as they had done on a couple of occasions. Well, what difference did it make? She might as well work. She noticed Patience still standing in front of her desk, and she hastily scribbled 'No' on the note and handed it back to the girl. 'Here, you can give this to Mr Simmons, please.'

Patience disappeared and Jacqueline could hear her clonking through the reception area in her platform shoes. She cleared her desk and picked up her shoulder-bag. First she wanted to go home and have something to eat. Matt was coming down the corridor towards her, walking with long, easy strides. She liked looking at him—the way he moved, the way he held his head, the way he smiled his lopsided smile. He wasn't handsome, but his rugged individuality held a strange attraction for her. And she was always aware of it.

'Well, if you have nothing better to do, how about some dinner away from Kwesi's magnificent cooking?'

He was asking her out to dinner! 'I'd like that.'

He frowned. 'Where's David? Is he out of town?'

'David? No, he's in Accra, I think.'

His frown grew deeper. 'Oh, well. Tell me, where'd you like to go?'

'Any place but the Goody-Goody Chop Bar.' It was a place not far from the office and sometimes the Ghanaian staff had lunch there.

Matt laughed. 'I wasn't thinking in that direction. How about something a little more extravagant?'

'I like the Commodore. I'd love some good Lebanese food—*houmous, tabouleh, kibbi.*'

'Okay. The Commodore it will be.'

He had not mentioned her birthday and Jacqueline was confused. Why was he taking her out?

She took great pains with her appearance, and the look of admiration he gave her was well worth the effort.

'You should wear your hair down more often,' he said. 'It's beautiful.'

Her hair fell in long soft waves down to her waist. The restaurant was air-conditioned and she didn't think it would be too hot. She felt like a teenager out on her first date and she couldn't understand why she felt shy and strangely pleased about his compliment.

Matt ordered wine with their meal, much to Jacqueline's horror. Ordinary wine was priced like champagne, but Matt only laughed at her protests.

'What's a birthday without a bottle of wine?'

So he had known!

'Oh, Matt, you knew all along!'

He laughed. 'Yes, from your personnel file. Last month when we discussed your new assignment I had to look something up because of the raise you got. That's when I noticed the date.' He put his hand in his pocket, took out a little package and pushed it across the table towards her. 'And here's a birthday present for the best AA in West Africa.'

She was too stunned to speak. She looked at the package, not touching it.

'Aren't you going to see what's inside?' he smiled.

'I can't accept it,' she protested.

'Don't tell me you even want to fight here, in a public place. What will all these people think?' he said in mock horror.

When she didn't answer him he picked up the package himself, opened the little box and put it next to her plate. 'This is a present from me to you. I want you to accept it. Please.'

Jacqueline lowered her eyes, looking in the little box.

Earrings. Small, delicate gold nuggets, products of age-old Ghanaian craftsmanship. Carefully she lifted them out and placed them on the palm of her hand.

'Oh, Matt!' she whispered.

Why? she thought. Why such an extravagant gift?

'Don't you like them?'

'Oh, Matt, they're lovely! They're beautiful!'

'And now I'd like to see them on you.' He took the earrings from her. 'And I want to put them on—this time.'

Memory made her flush. 'Oh, don't embarrass me! It's too dark in here anyway. You can't see well enough!'

'Wanna bet?' He came around the table and sat down on the chair next to her. 'Turn your face,' he commanded. His eyes were laughing into hers and she decided she'd better play along with him. Her hands reached up and took off the hoops she had in her ears.

He moved her hair away from her face. His hands were

cool against her warm cheek and his face was very close as he concentrated on the job. His nearness disturbed her; it always did. Every nerve in her body seemed aware of his presence and her heart fluttered crazily.

Matt worked quickly, deftly, and had no problem at all putting the earrings on. When he finished, he didn't move away, but looked at her appraisingly. 'You're beautiful. Especially with that blush on your cheeks.'

'I'm not blushing!'

'Oh, well. Must be the candlelight.' He went back to his own chair, lifted his wine glass. 'Happy birthday!'

'Thank you.' She was pleased and grateful and unaccountably happy. She touched the earrings, smiled at Matt. 'Why this present, Matt?'

'A peace-offering, because I was unforgivably stupid when you arrived here. And a thank-you for being nice to me when I needed someone to talk to that night I came home sloshed.'

'Thank you,' she said quietly. 'I'm ... pleased.' But she felt guilty, too. She hadn't been a model of virtue herself, leaving him in the dark about her background and experience until the résumé finally arrived.

'I'm glad.' He picked up his fork and began to eat.

Jacqueline scooped some *tabouleh* on to a leaf of lettuce, then put it back on her plate. 'Matt?'

'Yes?' He looked up, smiling. His eyes held hers.

'Matt, I ... I want to apologise.'

He raised his eyebrows. 'Apologise?'

'Yes. I haven't been very nice myself,' she said awkwardly. 'I mean, I should have told you about my experience. I just let you believe the wrong things because I was mad.'

'I know.' There was a deep, dark glitter in his eyes. 'But let's forget it. I know now what you really are.'

Jacqueline's heart skipped a beat. 'What's that?'

'You're damned good at your work. You're competent and efficient and you like what you're doing.' He paused. 'And I wouldn't want to lose you for the world.'

For all those months, this was what she had wanted him to think. And now he did. He had actually said so. And for some inexplicable reason she felt vaguely disappointed. What else, then, had she expected? she wondered.

'Let's forget the bad beginning,' said Matt. 'I like it better the way things have been going lately.'

'Yes.' She started eating again.

There weren't many people in the restaurant. The candles on the table created an intimate, romantic atmosphere and the wine made her feel light and carefree. Matt told her about his childhood—funny stories, sad stories, happy stories. She could have listened to him all night. The candles threw shadows on his face and his dark eyes gleamed at her as he talked. There were stirrings deep inside her, feelings and emotions she couldn't suppress. And she didn't want to. She didn't want to.

It was late when they finally came home. They entered the house and Matt opened the communicating door to her flat. She looked up to his face. He was so tall, so overpowering, overwhelming her with a longing she could hardly comprehend.

'I've had a wonderful evening, Matt. Thank you so much.'

His eyes were warm and smiling. 'It's quite all right. I enjoyed myself. You're nice company, Jackie.'

Neither of them moved. Jacqueline could feel the electricity, the vibrations between them. She lowered her eyes, fixing them on his bush-jacket, a silk-screen print of various greens. She wanted to put her face against his chest, feel his arms around her.

He gently lifted up her chin and his touch sent her

heart racing. Their eyes met. His gaze held tenderness and something else she couldn't define. Then, suddenly, his eyes changed, became dark and unreadable. He dropped his hand and turned away from her abruptly. 'Goodnight, Jackie.'

Don't leave me, she thought desperately. *Hold me! Kiss me!*

'Matt?' Her voice trembled oddly.

'Yes?' He turned and looked at her, the tenderness gone.

'Matt ... thank you for the lovely earrings.'

He smiled a crooked little smile. 'Sure, you're welcome.'

There was nothing else to do but close the door. She leaned against it, an acute sense of misery washing over her. Slowly she walked to the bathroom and looked in the mirror. Her face was sad and forlorn. The earrings shone softly in the light. For a long time she stared at her reflection, then she covered her face with her hands.

'No,' she whispered. 'Oh, no! Oh, no!'

She was in love with Matt. It was no use denying it any longer. Her feelings for him had slowly grown inside her, but up to now she'd been too afraid to acknowledge them for what they were—something deep and special and all-encompassing. Love.

It wasn't just his touch, his kisses that made her feel that way. She loved everything he stood for—the work he did, his feelings and beliefs, his integrity. He was not too proud to say sorry, to admit he had been wrong about her. He was a man of character and conviction, a strong man. His weaknesses—his stubbornness, his shortness of temper only made it more so.

Lying in bed she wondered why the reality of her feelings frightened her so much. Love was something joyous and wonderful, something to be happy about. But was it really always like that? *SWEET NOT ALWAYS.* The *tro-tro* slogan appeared before her mind's eye as if to answer her question. No, love was not always sweet.

What frightened her was that Matt did not love her. He liked her, yes. He appreciated her work, yes. He enjoyed her company, yes. And Tamale? A fleeting physical attraction at best. You couldn't call that love.

If only he loved her too! But in the days that followed he showed no signs of any deeper emotion. His friendly but somewhat distant manner hurt her and sometimes she almost wished they could go back to their old ways so she could lash back at him in anger.

'I'll be going on home leave soon,' Matt told her one morning. 'Can you arrange for my tickets?'

'Home leave?' she repeated, not sounding very intelligent. He had taken her by surprise.

'Yes, home leave.' He grinned. 'Don't you think I deserve some?'

'Yes, yes, of course.' She swallowed. Matt was leaving. He'd be gone for a whole month. Not so long ago she would have welcomed it, but now the thought alone seemed unbearable.

'Don't you want me to go?' He was smiling and she felt strangely confused looking at his face.

She pulled herself together, smiling back. 'Of course I want you to go. I just hadn't given much thought as to what we'll do while you're gone.'

'I'm sure you and our colleagues will manage admirably.'

'When are you going?' she asked.

'From the middle of September to the middle of October.' He gave her the details of his itinerary and left her to go back to his own office.

Some diversion arrived when Baba Minyila came to the office one day, accompanied by Connie, the clinic nurse. He was on business in Accra and was staying with one of his many relatives. He wanted to talk to Matt and offered his apologies for not having notified him in time of his arrival. Matt offered Connie the use of the guest room and Jacqueline abandoned her work to take the girl to the house.

Connie stayed for a week. It took her two days to get her medical supplies out of the harbour and she raged for days afterwards, Matt and Jacqueline having to listen again and again to every single detail of the ordeal. Although she had enjoyed Connie's lively company as a welcome distraction, Jacqueline let out a sigh of relief when finally she left. Matt grimaced and raised his eyes heavenward.

'Hallelujah!' he exclaimed.

'Oh, Matt!' Jacqueline couldn't help laughing. 'She's nice, really.'

'Maybe so, but she drove me crazy with her chatter.'

A week later David left for Kenya where he would be working for the next six or seven weeks. The last few weeks had been strange and disorganised and Jacqueline felt as though she were struggling through the days, feeling off balance and distracted.

There was an enormous amount of work to be done to get everything ready before Matt left, and often Jacqueline worked late. The more work, the better. She wanted her mind occupied so she wouldn't have time to think. At night she read herself to sleep. A box full of paperback books had arrived from home two days after her birthday—a present from her parents. They knew books were valuable property in a country where so little entertainment was available.

The day of Matt's departure arrived and Jacqueline drove him to the airport early in the morning. She watched the people while Matt stood in line to check in his luggage. A strange assortment of travellers had gathered in the lobby—Africans and Americans decked out in the most fantastic robes, dashikis, suits; Nigerian women with elaborately plaited hairdos; a group of Japanese athletes. Gold glittered in ears and around necks while luggage stood packed in wicker baskets and boxes tied with string. She could never be bored looking at people.

Matt came back from the check-in counter. 'God, what a madhouse!' he said irritably. They walked upstairs where more people stood in groups saying goodbye to the passengers.

Boarding time was announced and Matt grabbed his carry-on bag. 'Don't wait. We're bound to sit in the transit lounge for a while.'

'Okay. Have a nice vacation, Matt.' Mercifully, her voice sounded normal and didn't betray her inner turmoil.

He gave her a hasty smile, patted her on the shoulder. 'Good luck, Jackie. See you next month.' He strode through the gate, passport in hand. He didn't look at her again.

She watched him until he disappeared into the transit lounge. Then she turned, swallowing at the constriction in her throat. Slowly she walked to the balcony, paying her five pesewas to the girl guarding the entrance.

The plane looked enormous. Jacqueline stared at it for a long time while a strange melancholy slowly filled her. She was still standing there when the passengers began to board. She watched Matt walking along with long, even strides, going up the staircase, disappearing into the aircraft. Desolation washed over her and her eyes filled with tears.

You're an idiot, she told herself. A crazy, stupid idiot. She turned and walked out of the airport with everything blurred and colours dancing in front of her eyes.

She hadn't driven very far when she heard the plane thundering through the sky. The tears came freely then.

Jacqueline couldn't face the empty house or the office. At Danquah Circle she turned left and drove to Lisa's house.

'Good morning, Godson,' she said to the steward as she entered the kitchen. 'Is Mrs Turner home?'

'She's in the living-room, madame.'

Lisa was sitting on the couch going through a stack of magazines. She looked up when Jacqueline came in, pushing her glasses farther on to her nose. 'Hi. What are you doing here in the middle of the week during working hours? Did the chief fire you?'

'No.'

Lisa pushed the magazines aside. 'There's a recipe in one of these blasted magazines—you know, the kind that doesn't require fancy ingredients like cheese or green peas. But I can't find it.' She looked at Jacqueline quizzically. 'Have some coffee with me, okay?'

'I'd love some.'

Lisa went to the kitchen to give Godson his instructions. Coming back, she sat down again and looked at Jacqueline with a shrewd expression on her face.

'Well, isn't today the day the chief goes home on leave?'

'Yes. I just came back from the airport. I didn't feel like going to the office. I thought I'd celebrate my much-longed-for freedom with a cup of coffee with you.' Her voice sounded thin and there was an unmistakable lack of enthusiasm in her words.

'Very sensible indeed.'

Godson entered the room with a tray and Lisa rose to her feet and took it from him. 'Thanks, Godson.' She put the tray on the table and looked at Jacqueline. 'You take yours unadulterated, right?'

'Yes, just black, please.' She took the cup Lisa offered her. 'It's quiet here. Where's the baby?'

'Grace took her for a walk in the stroller. She always does right after breakfast, before it gets too hot.'

Lisa sat down again and took a careful sip of her coffee while she scrutinised Jacqueline.

'So what's the trouble?'

Jacqueline sighed. You couldn't fool Lisa.

'Considering all the given facts and evidence, wouldn't you say I should be glad Matt is out of my hair for a while?'

'Maybe.'

'What do you mean, *maybe*?'

'A while ago I should have said, yes, definitely, you should be jumping for joy to have him out of the way for a spell. But now I'm not so sure.' She paused. 'And it is rather obvious that you're not jumping for joy. In fact, I believe you've been crying.'

Jacqueline said nothing. She stared out the big windows where clouds of pink and orange bougainvillea blossoms hung in front of the glass. How much had Lisa guessed about her changing feelings for Matt?

'Jackie? Would you like to hear my diagnosis?'

She gave Lisa a half-smile. 'I'd like a second opinion.'

'All right, here goes. You're suffering from a heart condition spelled l-o-v-e. Hard, if not impossible to cure.' Lisa smiled. 'I've seen it coming for quite a while.'

A wave of misery washed over Jacqueline and she gave her friend a bitter smile. 'Couldn't be worse, could it? How stupid can you get?'

'Stupid hasn't got a thing to do with it. In fact, I think you're being extremely smart about it.'

'Oh?'

'You're not being stupid, ignoring the symptoms, pretending you dislike him when you don't, denying your true feelings. You've admitted the facts to yourself and now you can deal with them.'

'How? Tell me that!'

'First things first. What about Diane? She hasn't come back as far as I know. Is she still in the picture?'

Jacqueline shook her head. 'No, that's all over.'

'So then he's a free man?'

'Yes.'

'Then what's the problem?'

Jacqueline had always liked Lisa's direct approach, her straightforward manner, but now it bothered her. Lisa's analytical approach somehow took away from her feelings. As if, by looking at it critically, the situation could be reduced to a simple math problem: $a + b = c$. But love wasn't like that. At least not in her case.

'Then what's the problem?'

'Oh, Lisa, I don't know. I wish I knew.' She bent her head and put her face in her hands. 'I want him to love me back, but he doesn't. He just doesn't.'

'Jackie.' Lisa's voice was soft now. 'Jackie, I don't know anything about what happened between Matt and Diane. But whatever it was, it probably was painful. He was hurt. Give him some time to recuperate.'

Time. Jacqueline lifted her head and looked at Lisa. 'You think he might ... ?'

Lisa smiled and tipped her glasses farther on to her nose. '*NEVER DESPAIR*,' she said, quoting a *tro-tro* slogan. 'Just give him a chance to get himself together. If you really do love him, a little waiting won't hurt.'

A little waiting won't hurt. But the weeks of his absence dragged by. The atmosphere at the office was strangely dull, and the building seemed mysteriously empty. Everyone, it seemed, felt the lack of Matt's presence, as if he were the one who initiated all the activity and all the laughter. At first she tried to liven things up, but the staff showed an unmistakable lack of interest and enthusiasm, and Jacqueline eventually stopped trying.

She went to bed early, read for hours, more than she ever had before. A couple of times she had dinner with Lisa and John and that was the extent of her social life. If only David were here, she thought, but he was still in Nairobi, living it up. Everyone was having a good time, but her.

As if to make things worse, everything went wrong. Patience became ill and didn't come to work. The refrigerator gave up the ghost. The freezer was full of fish, guinea-fowl and rabbits, and Jacqueline ran around all Monday morning finding other freezing space. Lisa offered her freezer for part of the food and the rest went into David's after she'd spent two hours chasing the keys to his flat.

After repeated calls, the electricians finally arrived and dragged the refrigerator away on the back of a small pick-up truck painted with the colourful words: *Akujitu's Refrigeration—Fastest Service in Town.*

When, after a week, she still had no news from the fastest service in town, she drove up to the workshop to investigate.

'We are searching for the part,' Mr Azu told her, assuring her that half his crew had roamed the city day and night looking for it.

'Can you show me the broken part? Can you take it out?'

They presented her with the part.

'Now I'd like to take down all the specifications of the fridge. Model number, serial number, that sort of thing.' She climbed on a chair and wrote down the information she needed in her notebook.

Back in her office she composed a telegram to New York, requesting them to buy the part and give it to Matt to bring back. Lucky for him it wasn't a big piece.

Two weeks without a refrigerator. Well, she'd coped with worse problems. She sighed, looking at the stack of papers on her desk. She was late starting with the financial report.

She struggled for two days trying to make it balance, but to no avail. When she came home for lunch after an extremely frustrating morning, Kwesi announced that the iron had broken down and Jacqueline felt like screaming.

'I'll deal with it later,' she said, hastily swallowing her lunch. Back in the office she took the report and started over. By four o'clock it still didn't balance, but at least the difference was still the same—two cedis and fourteen pesewas.

She couldn't stand looking at another figure, so she walked out of the office in a fury. At home she grabbed the iron, wondering what to do. She recalled seeing a little electrical workshop by the road, not very far away. If she took the iron to The Fastest Service in Town, she wouldn't see it again for weeks.

She parked the car in the mud yard in front of the little wooden shack that boasted a blue sign informing the customer that the electrician was '*UK Trained.*' The little shack hung together more by luck than design. The floorboards creaked under her feet as she entered. The electrician sat on a stool behind a rickety table and started to work on the iron immediately. Jacqueline sat down on a chair and nearly fell over backwards. The chair hung loosely together and the back was attached rather casually with two rusty nails.

While the electrician with his round shiny face and his Donald Duck T-shirt took apart her iron, Jacqueline surveyed the place. The wooden doors were painted light blue, the walls green, the shelves pink. There was a general veneer of dust and dirt over everything and on the shelves a few mysterious-looking parts were spending their old age. Some dusty light-bulbs were available too, but most likely not working.

'A loose wire,' the man said. 'Very dangerous.' Swiftly he put the iron back together again and tested it on a contraption with red and green lights. He let her feel the warm surface and smiled. 'Fixed.'

She thought of the sign outside.

'You've been in England, right?'

He smiled. 'Yes.'

'How long were you there?'

'Two weeks.'

'You took an electrician's course in *two weeks*?'

'Oh no. I was on a ship.'

'A ship? Were you trained on a ship?'

'No. We took lumber to England and I was working in the kitchen. We spent two weeks in London before we came back.'

For a moment Jacqueline was speechless. 'You mean you never took a course in England?'

He grinned. 'No.'

'But it says "*UK Trained*" on the sign outside.'

A mischievous look came into his eyes and his grin widened. 'Oh, well, you know—*Advertising*!'

Jacqueline laughed out loud. It would make a wonderful story to tell Matt when he came back. Matt. Always Matt. She wished she could stop thinking about him, but he was in the back of her mind all the time.

The financial report was long overdue now and she took it home with her that night to work on it. She sat at the big dining room table covered with papers and went through every single number once more. It had to be some stupid little mistake, somewhere.

She found it on Matt's expense report.

The numbers blurred in front of her eyes. Oh, Matt, she thought in desperation, can't you even leave me alone when you're away? She pushed the papers aside and put her head on her arms and cried.

David made it back to Ghana one week before Matt was due, bearing gifts of Kenya coffee, cheese, and a piece of Maridadi cloth. And a great big bear-hug that left Jacqueline breathless.

'Oh, David, you shouldn't have!'

'Oh yes, I should! The cloth is a bribe. I want you to fix some of that delectable cheese soufflé and some real perked coffee and then invite me to dinner. Not tonight, of course.' He flashed her a charming smile.

Jacqueline held out the cloth to look at the design, the dazzling colours. 'It's gorgeous, David. Quite different from the market cloth here, isn't it?'

'There's an entire continent in between Ghana and Kenya,' he grinned, a teasing look in his eyes.

She felt an infantile desire to stick out her tongue, but didn't. 'I'm quite aware of that. I was just making an observation.' She folded the cloth and put it down. 'Can I get you something to eat? There isn't much because we haven't a fridge at the moment.'

'Nope, nothing. I came here to invite you to dinner and then I'll tell you all about my trip. I shot three lions, was charged by an elephant and almost got swallowed by a hippo.'

Jacqueline laughed. 'You forgot the snakes and the baboons.' She shook her head. 'Sorry, David, but those fantastic stories work better at home where you have a more gullible audience.'

'Spoilsport!'

'Is Kenya really as beautiful as they say?'

'It's gorgeous, fascinating, intriguing, and yes, beautiful. Come on, make yourself pretty and let's go.'

Matt's plane was late. Jacqueline was waiting for it to arrive and she couldn't remember ever having been so nervous. The airport was crowded and noisy and had a general atmosphere of confusion. It was hot, sticky and uncomfortable, even out on the balcony where usually it was quite breezy.

Finally the plane arrived and Jacqueline strained her eyes looking at the passengers coming down the stairs and walking into the terminal. No Matt. Where was he? She waited until every last one of the passengers had come through Customs. The airport was almost deserted when she finally gave up. He wasn't there. He hadn't been on the plane. Disappointment welled up inside her and she walked back to her car, feeling miserable and let down. There wasn't another flight from New York until next week.

Two nights later she woke up, hearing someone calling and tapping on the outside of her air-conditioner. 'Jackie! It's me, Matt! Let me in, please.'

Hastily she groped for her robe. It wasn't there. In the laundry? Never mind. She ran to the door, her heart pounding against her ribs.

'Matt!' The moment she saw him, a wave of such longing washed over her, she felt faint and dizzy.

'I'm sorry I had to wake you up, but I didn't have my key and Kwesi isn't home.' He moved past her into her sitting room.

'It doesn't matter,' she said. And it didn't. She wanted to go to him, hold him, feel his body against hers. But he didn't stop. He walked straight through the connecting door into the main room and dumped his suitcases on the floor without giving her another look. She followed him in.

'Matt, where are you coming from?'

'London, by Caledonian.'

'*London?*'

'I had a meeting with some bank people about funding the programme. It came up at the last moment and there wasn't time to let you know. I'm sorry you came to the airport for nothing on Tuesday.'

'It doesn't matter.'

He rubbed his neck. 'God, what a flight! I was supposed to be here hours ago, but just as we were landing the lights at the airport went out. We flew to Abidjan and waited for more than an hour until they had the lights fixed.'

He looked exhausted.

'Anything I can get you, Matt? Something to drink?'

'No, thanks. I just want to go to bed.' He looked at her, not really seeing her. 'How did things go here?'

'Fine. No great problems.'

'Well, I'm going to shower and go to bed. We'll talk tomorrow.' He turned and stalked out of the room.

Jacqueline sat on the couch, not able to move. He had scarcely looked at her and she wished she could deny the feelings of desperation inside her. What had she expected? Certainly not a passionate embrace.

She didn't know how long she'd been sitting there when the door opened and Matt came back into the living room, wearing a cotton dressing gown and thongs.

'You're still here? I thought you'd gone back to bed.'

'I'm not sleepy.' Her heart pounded wildly when he sat down next to her.

'I'm not either. The shower revived me and I got my second wind.' He raked his hand through his hair and smiled. 'I was going to get myself a drink. Want one?'

'There's nothing cold, but I'll have a sherry.'

'I guess I can stand a straight Scotch without ice. By the way, I have the part for the refrigerator.'

He brought the glasses and sat down again. 'So, no great tragedies happened in my absence?'

'No, just little ones. Patience was sick for a week. The fridge broke down. The iron stopped working. And it took me three days to balance the financial report.' She didn't add that it had been his fault.

'Was that all? Sure you didn't forget something?' He laughed and she couldn't bear looking in his eyes. Her blood was throbbing in her ears. With an unsteady hand she brought the glass to her lips and drank some of the sherry.

'Are you all right? Jackie, you're shaking!' He took the glass from her and put it down. He lifted up her face. 'What's happened? Is something wrong?'

'Nothing.' Her heart was pounding so hard, she was sure he had to hear it. She was overwhelmed with longing for him, his arms, his mouth. Emotions too strong to fight came welling up from deep inside her. She closed her eyes.

'Matt ... kiss me ... kiss me.' It came out in a low whisper. All self-control left her and she could no longer resist her feelings of need for him. Her arms went around him, holding him. She lifted her face and his mouth came down on hers. He kissed her with a sudden, drunken passion that left nothing to the imagination. He wanted her as much as she wanted him. Her mind was empty of thought and reasoning and all she felt were waves of love and longing so acute they were almost like physical pain. Through the thin material of her nightgown she felt his body, hard and wanting. She clung to him in wild, uncontrollable desire, until suddenly, cruelly, he pushed her from him.

'What the hell do you think you're doing!'

The world was spinning around her and his words cut like ice through her mind. She could feel all colour draining from her face. Horrified at her helpless passion, she stared at him. His face was hard, his eyes dark and cold.

She was shaking under his stare and she felt sick with shame. Words stuck in her throat. There was nothing she could say or do to wipe out the preceeding minutes and she wanted to run, or die, or sink into the ground.

Matt stood up from the couch, towering over her. 'Thanks for the offer, but no, thanks.' And with that he left the room.

CHAPTER EIGHT

JACQUELINE lay in bed, not knowing how she got there. She was trembling with humiliation and there was an ache in her chest that seemed to rip her apart. Tears were sliding down her cheeks on to the pillow. Oh, God, she thought, what did I do! How can I face him again after this?

But there was no choice. She had to face him again. Working in his office, living in his house, there was no way to avoid him.

It was three o'clock. She was jittery and nervous and she couldn't relax enough to go to sleep. His words kept coming back to her, haunting her. *'Thanks for the offer, but no, thanks!'* What had he been thinking? Nice girls don't throw themselves at men. But nice had nothing to do with it. She loved him and his attraction was overpowering. She had no resistance to it. I couldn't help myself, she thought desperately. I couldn't help myself! She was crying again, hiding her face in the pillow.

At four o'clock the first chickens started cackling, although it wouldn't be light for another two hours. Jacqueline huddled under the sheet, trying to block out the noise. A restless slumber finally took over and she awoke from it exhausted. She dragged herself out of bed and looked in the bathroom mirror. There were circles under her eyes and she looked ill. Would Matt be at the breakfast table? Her face looked back at her with nervous anticipation. Involuntarily, her hands clenched into fists.

You will go out there and wish him a good morning.

*And then you will sit down across the table from him
and eat your breakfast and make small talk. Keep your
head high. Look him squarely in the face.*

Keep her head high. But all she wanted to do was
crawl under the sheet and hide—never, never see him
again.

She showered and dressed, taking special care to
camouflage her washed-out appearance with make-up
With her stomach tied in knots and her legs trembling,
she opened the communicating door and entered the
main room.

Matt was not there. In the kitchen she found Kwesi
frying eggs.

'Did you see Mr Simmons?' she asked.

'Mr Simmons?' Kwesi looked baffled. 'He is home?'

Of course, Kwesi didn't know Matt had come back in
the night. And of course Matt wasn't going to get up at
the normal hour. Not after coming back from London. A
sigh of relief escaped her. At least the confrontation
would be postponed until later.

Fit and fresh, with no sign of fatigue, he came striding into her office a few hours later. There was a faint
whiff of after-shave and her heart lurched at the sight of
him.

His face was expressionless. 'Good morning.' His voice
was cool and calm. 'My in-box looks somewhat over-
whelming. I'd like you to give me a hand with it and fill
me in on some of the priorities.'

'I'll be with you in a minute.'

This was business. Neutral ground. 'Shall I bring some
coffee?'

'Please.'

Jacqueline didn't know how she managed to keep her
composure, how she looked at him and talked to him as
if nothing had happened. But somehow she succeeded.

The weeks passed by in a dull haze and she worked frantically, trying not to think. It was as if she moved through the days fully anaesthetised, not feeling anything. It was the only way she managed to cope at all.

At meal times they sat across the table from each other, silently, or making meaningless small talk. Matt didn't seem to notice her change of behaviour, or maybe he wanted it that way, too. They were like polite strangers asking or wanting nothing from each other. The barrier between them seemed there to stay and Jacqueline felt dead and empty inside.

But in unguarded moments she would find herself staring at him, at his strong, tanned fingers signing letters, at his hair curling around his ears, and a shaft of pain would shoot through her. She knew she didn't hate him, could never hate him. But what on earth had possessed her that night he came back from London? What had made her think, or even hope, he would feel the same way about her?

Love. What had she expected? As a young girl she had dreamed of a wine and moonlight romance. Roses and kisses and holding hands in the dark. Her daydreams had been filled with images of knights in armour, handsome princes, Grecian demi-gods. Later she had hoped for a man who was a partner—a man who would love her and respect her for what she was, who would look beyond the blonde, blue-eyed exterior and see what lay beneath it, and value it.

'*I know what you are.*' Matt had said those words when he had taken her to dinner on her birthday. But what was it that he knew? He knew her as a good worker—not as a woman. He hadn't said anything about that. He wasn't interested in her as a woman. And still he had kissed her and held her with both tenderness and passion. He hadn't been indifferent, she knew.

The more Jacqueline thought about it, the more confused she became. What had she done wrong?

The only thing she was sure of, the only thing that didn't change was her love for him. She loved him with a desperation she herself didn't understand. He was the man she wanted, the man she wanted to share her life with. His enthusiasm about his work, his concern for the people he worked with never failed to amaze her. His life had a sense of purpose. He was out there struggling, fighting, helping people. He was a man of compassion.

But there was more to it than that. He was a man in every sense of the word. He aroused in her feelings she had never felt for any other man. His touch sent her senses clamouring for more and more and more.... Her love felt like a deep ache inside her and she closed her eyes, switching her mind off forbidden thoughts. She'd have to learn to live without it, without him.

Sensing something was wrong, David tried to talk to her. They were in his apartment, where he'd had a small dinner party. Now the guests had gone and they were alone, drinking another glass of wine.

'You're not fooling me, Jackie. I know something is wrong. It's as if the life has gone out of you.'

'I can't talk about it,' she said miserably, wishing she hadn't had any wine. It didn't do her any good in the state she was in.

'I'm your friend, Jackie.'

'David, I ... I....' To her horror her voice wobbled and her cool and calm composure crumbled. Matt's face floated through her mind. She saw his mop of dark hair, his crooked nose, his crazy lopsided smile. His voice came to her from nowhere ... 'You're beautiful. You're beautiful in a very special way.' She could feel his arms again, his lips on hers.

But they were not Matt's arms now. They were David's. 'Jackie, Jackie.' He held her against him, stroking her hair.

I'm not going to cry, she thought fiercely. I am *not* going to cry. Her throat ached with the effort and her eyes burned. After a while she relaxed, her head on David's shoulder, knowing she shouldn't be there, not caring.

Finally she raised her head.

'I'm sorry, David, it's the wine. I can't take it—it does things to me.'

'Don't apologise.' He brushed the hair from her face and bent down to kiss her. She did not resist. If only it were Matt, she thought. If only it were Matt holding her, kissing her, telling her it was all some terrible nightmare and he loved her.

But it wasn't Matt kissing her. It was David. David who had been nice to her all along, who had been a friend to her, who was kind and understanding now. If only she loved him, everything would be so simple. But she didn't love David—not the way a woman should love a man.

She moved away from him. 'David, I have to go home now.'

'Why don't you stay, Jackie?'

The temptation was there, fleetingly. Yes, why not? There weren't many men like David. He would be nice and gentle and she liked him and he liked her.

But that had never been enough and it wasn't enough now.

'I can't stay, David. It wouldn't be fair.'

'Oh, Jackie, you're the stubbornest woman I've ever known!' He smiled, shaking his head. 'Come on, I'll take you home.'

Sitting beside David in the car, driving through the

dark silent night, she knew something had to happen soon. She couldn't live day in and day out with this terrible emptiness inside her.

She asked David to let her out at the gate and he wished her goodnight, kissing her lightly on the cheek. Ali closed the gates behind her and she walked slowly up the path to her flat. As she entered her sitting room, the connecting door flew open and Matt stood towering in the doorway, glaring. Suddenly the air was heavy with tension.

'Where the hell have you been?' The question shot through the silence, hitting her like a physical blow. She looked at Matt, steadying herself.

'It's none of your business!'

'Well, I suppose I can guess,' he said savagely, looking her up and down, taking in her long dress, her dangling earrings. 'Wining and dining again! It's two o'clock on a Wednesday night!'

Jacqueline winced at the tone of his voice. 'Well, if you'll excuse me, I'll go to bed now.' She started for the bedroom, but he caught her by the arm and yanked her to a standstill. Enraged, she pulled herself away.

'Let me go!'

They stared at each other in fury, the air between them electric with tension, sparks flying.

'There was a phone call for you less than an hour ago,' he said in a low, controlled voice. 'At one o'clock, to be exact. I went looking for you, but you were not in your bed.'

Fear shot through her. A phone call in the middle of the night spelled disaster. A call from the U.S.? Had something happened to her parents, her grandmother?

'Who was it?' she asked anxiously.

'I don't know. He didn't tell me his name, and I think he was drunk. One of your loony boy-friends, probably.

By the time I came back to the phone, he'd had second thoughts and hung up.'

Relief washed over her. If it had been an international phone call, he would have known it.

'Well, I'm sorry you were disturbed at that hour,' she said.

His eyes shot fire at her. 'That's not exactly the problem. The problem was the fact that you were not in your bed! For all I knew you could be lying in a gutter somewhere, run over by some maniacal taxi driver! Can't you imagine what I was thinking?'

No, she couldn't. There were a variety of other places she could have been besides bleeding to death in a gutter. David's bed, for instance.

'I'm deeply touched by your concern, but now I'd like to go to sleep.'

Without another word he turned on his heel and walked out of the room, slamming the door so it rang through the house.

One Saturday afternoon in the middle of November Jacqueline sat on her verandah, trying to read. But the book couldn't keep her attention. Her eyes kept moving to the colour in the garden, the bougainvilleas, the scarlet hibiscus, the frangipani. How she had loved this place! And how much of the shine had gone off everything. She moved through the days like a wind-up doll, trying not to feel, or think, just doing the things that had to be done. Nothing seemed to matter. But at times like this, when she was alone with herself, not working, not having anything else to keep her occupied, the questions came haunting her.

Why did she love Matt? Why was it so hard to stop it and forget it? Love was supposed to give joy, make you deliriously happy, but it wasn't doing any such thing to her. *SWEET NOT ALWAYS.* For her, love was bitter and a constant ache in her chest. It was growing worse every time she saw him, or heard his voice, or thought about him. Would it ever go away?

Kwesi's chickens cackled loudly and flew up on the little wall separating the garden from the neighbour's. From somewhere came the dull thudding of someone pounding *fufu*. The gate squeaked and a car drove up the drive. It was David, grinning widely, blond hair shining. He looked outrageous in his embroidered purple shirt, cut-off blue jeans and plastic thongs.

'Hi there, beautiful. Are you busy?'

She shook her head. 'No, please sit down. Would you like something cold to drink? Water? Iced tea? We haven't been able to get beer lately.'

'Iced tea sounds fine.'

Glad for the distraction, she jumped up and went to the kitchen to get the pitcher and glasses.

'I have news for you,' David said when she came back. 'And you're the first to know.'

'Tell me, tell me.'

'I'm being promoted and transferred to the Philippines.'

She stared at him with open mouth. '*The Philippines?*'

'Yep, leaving next month.'

'Oh, David!' A sinking feeling of dejection overwhelmed her.

'Aren't you happy for me?'

'Yes, oh yes! It's just ... it's so far away. I'll miss you.'

'I'll miss you too, Jackie.'

They stared at each other gravely. Jacqueline swallowed painfully.

'David, what went wrong?' Her voice was very low and he looked at her for a long moment.

'Nothing went wrong, Jackie. It just didn't happen for us.'

'I wish it had,' she sighed.

'So do I.'

'I wish I loved you. I'd go to the Philippines with you and. . . .'

'And we'd live happily ever after?' His eyes shone with amusement.

She smiled and nodded. 'I'm silly, I know.'

'If you wanted to come, I'd let you.'

Surprised, she stared at him. 'You would?'

David nodded. 'Yes, with one or two concessions on your part. And it would be the stupidest thing we ever did.' Suddenly he smiled wickedly. 'But I'd enjoy it as long as it lasted—two weeks, three.'

'Oh, David!'

And they were laughing again.

Then the farewell parties began. Jacqueline was invited to most of them, and so was Matt. They went their separate ways to the parties and back as if they lived miles apart. She had Thanksgiving dinner at Lisa's house and she didn't know where Matt was spending the evening.

One of David's friends owned a cottage at the beach and gave a party there. It was a lavish affair with battery-operated lamps lighting the beach and lots of expensive French foods imported from Togo. There was music and singing and dancing all around. Some of the people had brought their swimming suits and went out in the surf to swim and play.

Jacqueline had put on her bikini too and given the sea a hesitant try-out. She didn't like swimming at night; it was too dark and the undercurrents were bad. She didn't like the party. It was dangerous to have people drinking and swimming at the same time, especially at night. She didn't know many of the guests and she was in no mood to acquaint herself with any of them. She hadn't been in the mood for anything lately. She moved away from the people and the lights and the laughter and sat down on a log near the water. It was much too dark to walk very far, and she was too tired, anyway. Too tired even to think. Numbness took over as she stared at the dark sea, hearing the waves splashing loudly on the beach, the foamy froth of the waves glowing strangely in the moon-light.

She sensed more than saw someone coming towards her. Not until he had come very close did she recognise the tall figure towering darkly over her.

'Jacqueline?'

Matt! Her heart lurched in panic. There was nothing to be afraid of, she told herself. It was only Matt.

'Yes?'

He sat down beside her on the log. 'I want to talk to you.'

'This is a party and I'm trying to relax. I'm not in-terested.'

'I'm not here to talk business, dammit!'

She didn't answer. Every nerve in her body tightened itself. Her heart bounced around like a ping-pong ball gone crazy.

'You haven't looked at me or talked to me for weeks! I haven't had a chance to be alone with you without someone lurking in the background! Kwesi, or Patience, or somebody.'

'I don't want to be alone with you!' She didn't recog-nise her own voice as she spoke, but there was fear and anger in her words.

'Well, *I* want to be alone with *you*!' He took her by the shoulders and yanked her against his chest. His arms went around her and before she knew what was happening, he was kissing her hard on the mouth. She could feel his bare skin against hers and a wave of panic surged through her. She couldn't let it happen, not again. Violently she jerked her face away.

'Don't touch me! Don't you ever touch me again!' But his arms were still around her and he didn't let her go. Memory washed over her again and with it the deep humiliation of that night when he had returned from London. Her senses left her and there was nothing now but the pain and the agony of that night and the rising hysteria his touch invoked in her. She didn't want him to touch her. *She didn't want him to touch her!*

'Let me go!' she screamed. 'Let me go!' She struggled against the steely strength of his arms, but his grip tightened.

'Stop it Jackie! Stop it, stop it!' He had taken her shoulders and was shaking her, shaking. Strange shudders were going through her and she knew she was sobbing, but she couldn't stop herself. The sea was roaring in her ears and in one last desperate lurch she freed herself—or did he let her go? Stumbling, she ran away from him, blindly groping her way through the dark, back to the cottage.

She opened doors, found a bedroom, threw herself across one of the beds, sobbing hysterically. The next moment David was standing beside the bed looking down on her with a shocked expression on his face.

'Jackie! For God's sake, what's happened?'

'Nothing,' she said, turning her face away from him. 'Nothing. Please leave me alone, David.'

'You come in here crying as if the world has come to an end and you tell me nothing has happened?'

There was a lamp on the table and he moved it closer to look at her better. 'What is this?' His fingers touched her shoulder, and she looked down and saw the red marks Matt's grip had left. Under his searching eyes, she felt strangely naked in her bikini.

'It's nothing ... it's....'

'Did somebody try something, Jackie? Tell me!'

'No, no! It's not what you think! It's not like that at all! David....' There was a knock on the door and Jacqueline jerked herself upright. 'Don't let him in, David! Don't let him in!'

In one agile movement he was out of the room. She heard voices, loud and excited and then lower and lower. She couldn't hear a word of what was being said. She lay back on the pillow, every nerve and muscle tensed. It seemed a long time before David came back into the room, alone.

'Well, are you ready for a shot of whisky?'

'Yes, yes, please.'

He handed her a glass with some Scotch in it and she sipped it slowly, not looking at him.

'Was that Matt at the door?'

There was a silence before he answered. 'Yes, it was.'

'It wasn't what you thought, David.'

'No, I know.'

She wondered what they had been saying, but obviously David wasn't going to tell her. She didn't care. She didn't care.

The whisky had calmed her down. She told David she was all right and he left her to go back to the party. She turned off the light and stared into the dark, seeing nothing but the tiny glowing point of the mosquito coil David had lighted. A breeze touched the curtains and the fragrance of the mosquito coil filled her nostrils. Outside the music continued, and the singing and the laughing.

I'll have to go, she thought. I can't take this any more. I'll have to leave and find another job or ask for a transfer. I can't live like this and feel myself grow cold and empty.

Later, David came back into the room and handed her her clothes. 'It's time to go. I'll take you home.'

She shook her head. 'No. I have one of the office cars here. I didn't come with Matt.'

'Tomorrow is Sunday. We can come back and pick it up. But you're coming with me now.' He left her to get dressed.

It was a long drive home, but David never said a single word.

David left the week before Christmas with the promise to visit Jacqueline's parents in the States. She wished she could go too, if only to be away from Accra and Matt. She didn't know how she was going to live through the next few weeks until she'd had a reply from New York to her request and could tell Matt about her transfer.

The *harmattan* had arrived and the northern winds clouded the sky with a grey-yellow dust, obscuring the sun. The heat was unbearable and her nose and throat ached with the dust. The atmosphere was depressing and did nothing for Jacqueline's state of mind. The sun was a dull golden ball barely visible through the dust clouds, and she thought it symbolised her life—no shine, no glow, no love.

The Turners had planned a big Christmas dinner party with Turkey flown in from Kenya, and Jacqueline helped Lisa with the preparations.

'I know it's none of my business,' Lisa said as they were busy in the kitchen making the stuffing, 'but I can't help noticing the change that's come over you.'

'It's the *harmattan*,' she said lightly. 'You know what it does to people. It changes their personalities. They go crazy.'

'Baloney!' Lisa looked at her, frowning. 'You've lost weight. You're unhappy, edgy, and closed like a clam-shell. What happened between you and Matt?'

For a moment Jacqueline said nothing, staring stupidly at the box of dried thyme in her hands. Then something snapped inside her and the words came spilling out.

'Oh, Lisa! Everything's all wrong. I've been so stupid and ... and I've decided to leave. I can't take it any more. I've got to get out of here.' So it was out. She'd told somebody, and why not? Lisa was her friend.

'You are *what*?' Lisa's hands dropped to the counter and she looked at Jacqueline with wide eyes.

'I'm going to resign.'

'Why?'

'I can't take being around Matt any more. He ... he doesn't want me. It's been impossible these last two months. We don't get along and we're always fighting.' She could feel the tears welling up in her eyes, slowly dripping down her cheeks. She didn't care.

'You love him, Jackie.'

'I know. I know! But he doesn't want me!'

'Come on, let's sit down.' Lisa put her arm around Jacqueline's shoulders and led her into the living-room. 'Now tell me. What happened?'

'He thinks I'm some sort of cheap girl out on the make.'

'Why would he think that?'

'Well ... oh, Lisa, I'm too embarrassed. It was awful!'

'Tell me anyway.'

And so she did. It all came tumbling out, one word on top of another and all the time she was talking she didn't look at Lisa, but stared out the window at the bougain-villea blossoms against the glass. After she was finished, Lisa didn't say anything for a long time.

Finally Lisa sighed. 'Maybe,' she said slowly, 'you'd better tell Matt you want to leave.'

Jacqueline looked unseeingly at her hands that lay clenched in her lap. There were visions of Matt's face floating through her mind. She bit her lip and nodded miserably. 'I'll tell him after I hear from New York.'

Jacqueline's request for a transfer to Niger had not been received with great enthusiasm by the people in the head office. Jacqueline's hands shook as she read through the letter. 'We need you in Ghana. You're doing an excellent job and we wouldn't want to lose you.' She knew all that, even though it was nice to see it in black and white. But she simply couldn't stay and she hoped they were taking her request seriously. She read on and felt reassured. Since the programme in Niger had expanded considerably in the last year, there was a need to add on to the staff, and Jacqueline with her Ghana experience and knowledge of French certainly would fill the bill.

But please, the letter said, would she reconsider her request, since it would be an added burden to Matt to train someone new.

I don't care, Jacqueline thought bitterly. Let him suffer a little. Good for him!

'We don't know what the problem is,' the letter concluded, 'but if there is anything we can do from this end, please let us know.'

Well, there was nothing they could do about her problems here, but they could use her in Niger and they would transfer her there if she didn't change her mind. It was all she needed to know. She put the letter back in its envelope and let out a deep sigh of relief.

Now she had to tell Matt. The thought alone made her feel warm and uncomfortable, but she had the rest of the afternoon to think about it. Matt was spending the day at the goat project and wouldn't be back until seven or eight.

Jacqueline had an early dinner and afterwards settled herself in her sitting-room with a book and a cup of coffee. But she couldn't read. She was jittery and nervous and every time a car turned the corner her heart skipped a beat.

As she sat there thinking, she suddenly realised with a clarity she had not before perceived, that this was the end. Going to Niger would terminate it all, put out every spark of hope she might have secretly nursed. He'd be out of her life and she'd never see him again. Of course, through the company grapevine she would hear about him, know where he was, what he was doing.

She pictured herself in Niger. A new country, a new office, a new boss. A new beginning. I'll be miserable, she thought. I'll cry my heart out ... for a while. Luckily, in a desert climate, tears dry fast, she told herself in a half-hearted attempt at humour. But it wasn't funny. The loneliness she would feel would be hard to bear, but nothing could be worse than the intolerable situation she was coping with now.

Well, she'd always wanted to see the desert, hadn't she? Here was her opportunity. Niger was mostly desert —lots of sand and camels and Tuaregs. But no matter how she tried, Jacqueline couldn't conjure up any enthusiasm for her new experiences. The appeal of new and exciting adventures had vanished. Without love, nothing really mattered.

When finally Matt came home, she had almost persuaded herself to wait until the next day to speak to him, but she knew it would only make it harder. Well, at least she could give him enough time to have something to eat. When finally she ventured into the main living-room, she found him sitting at the dining table, papers spread out in front of him. He seemed absorbed in his work and apparently was not aware of her presence.

Flurries of high-life music drifted through the open windows, mingling with the incessant chirping of the crickets. Her heart pounding wildly, she took a deep breath trying to calm herself.

'Matt, I'd like to talk to you.'

He looked up from his papers impatiently. 'Yes, what is it?'

Irritation replaced her nervousness and she looked at him defiantly.

'I'm handing in my resignation. I've asked for a transfer and they're considering me for Niger.'

A dead silence followed her words. Disbelief and surprise raced across his face. Then something else flickered in his eyes. Anger? Fear? She wasn't sure.

'You're *what?*' His voice exploded in the silence and she winced at the violence of his tone.

'You heard me. I hope you're pleased. You never wanted me, and now I'm leaving.'

'Oh no, you're not!'

'Oh yes, I am!'

The air was electric with tension. They were at it again, facing each other in fury and frustration. This time she hadn't expected it. It would always be the same, she thought bitterly.

Matt straightened his back. 'May I ask you why?'

'Because of us.'

'Us?'

'Yes, us. You and me. We don't get along. We don't understand each other. We're always fighting and it's getting on my nerves. I've no intention of becoming a neurotic because of you!' Anger grew hotter and hotter inside her as she talked. Her legs were weak and shaky.

'You don't need me! Surely you can find someone to re-
place me. Even I don't think I'm indispensable! But I do
have my pride!'

'I don't want you to leave.' He sounded strangely calm
and quiet.

Jacqueline took a deep breath. 'Give me *one* good
reason why I should stay!' Her voice was high with
anger and her legs wouldn't stop trembling.

For a moment it was very quiet. His eyes, dark and
unreadable, held hers.

'Because I love you.'

The world was spinning around her. Oh no, he
wouldn't do that! He wouldn't lower himself to such
dirty tactics, using her feelings to manipulate her into
staying! Dizziness took hold of her and she couldn't
focus her eyes. She groped for the back of a chair,
steadied herself and forced her eyes to his face.

'Oh, no, Matt,' she said in a low, level voice. 'Oh, no.
Don't try that on me.'

CHAPTER NINE

She turned, ran out of the house, passed Ali, got into the car. It was as though she were in a trance, not really knowing what she was doing, just moving her body, letting out the clutch, pushing in the accelerator. She didn't know where she was going. All she knew was that she had to get away from Matt and from the devastating reality that lay behind his words—the reality that he had mocked her deepest feelings, that he was not the man she'd thought he was.

Her hands tightened on the steering wheel. All he cared about was keeping her on the job. It would be a headache for him to break in someone new. '*I wouldn't want to lose you for the world.*' The words suddenly hammered through her brain. He had told her that the night of her birthday. '*I wouldn't want to lose you for the world.*' But she wasn't stupid enough to fall for his ploy. He wasn't going to manipulate her into doing what he wanted her to do; be used.

It wasn't safe driving blinded by tears—she'd kill somebody. She had to go some place, talk to someone. Lisa. She could go to Lisa. She prayed she would be home.

She was. And so was John.

Jacqueline sank down on the sofa, clenching her hands into fists, trying desperately to calm herself.

'Jackie! What's happened?' There was a worried, urgent tone to Lisa's voice, but Jacqueline couldn't talk. Her throat was locked and the words wouldn't come. Lisa's face was a blur. John pressed a glass in her hand and she noticed she was shaking.

'Here, drink this,' he said. 'Don't talk.'

Slowly she sipped the whisky and after a while she felt the calming effects spread through her body. She realised that John had left the room and that she was alone with Lisa.

'You want to talk about it?'

'I ... I think so.'

'I don't need any preliminaries. You told him you're resigning, right?'

'Yes.'

'And he wasn't particularly enthusiastic about the idea?'

'No....' She swallowed. 'How did you guess?'

Lisa smiled. 'Just a hunch. Did he tell you why?'

Jacqueline nodded miserably, clenching her fists, feeling tears come back into her eyes. 'He said ... he said that he didn't want me to leave because ... because he loves me.' She closed her eyes. 'He's using me, Lisa. He knows how I feel about him. He must have figured it out and now he's taking advantage of it....'

'Not so long ago he thought you were a cheap girl out on the make—at least that's what you told me.'

Jacqueline buried her head in her hands. 'I don't know, Lisa. I don't understand it any more. He acts so strangely sometimes, I never know what to make of him.' The tears were trickling through her fingers. Images of Matt's face floated through her mind—hard and angry, friendly and smiling.

At times he had laughed at her and purposely made her mad. He had looked at her in contempt and on that horrible night in October he had said the most cruel words of all. *'What the hell do you think you're doing! Thanks for the offer, but no, thanks!'* The words still hurt, would always hurt. No matter what might become of her, she would never forget them.

But there had been other times, too. Times when he had teased her without malice, smiled at her, held her in his arms and kissed her. He had given her gold earrings, thanking her for being nice to him. He had been honest and sincere, she was sure of that. All of it had changed that night he had come back from England. Why? *Why?*

She raised her face and looked at Lisa. 'I don't know, Lisa. It's all such a muddled-up mess. I've thought and thought about it, but I can't begin to comprehend it.'

'Jackie, did it ever occur to you that Matt might have meant what he said tonight?'

Jacqueline stared at Lisa, dumbfounded. 'No,' she said in a whisper.

Lisa shook her head impatiently. 'See?' she said with a touch of aggravation in her voice. 'See? That's what I mean! You're lashing out at each other. You don't believe for a moment he might mean what he says. It didn't even occur to you! No, you automatically assume the opposite! You're wrapped up in some crazy pattern of fighting and hurting each other. Everything good between you is buried under a pile of misunderstandings. You can't even see the truth any more. It's sick, Jackie! And you're a fool!'

For a moment Lisa's tirade left Jacqueline speechless.

'Thanks,' she said drily. 'Thanks for the comfort and the sympathy. Just what I needed.'

'Oh, Jackie!' Lisa's voice had softened. 'I can't stand by and watch the two of you ruin your own and each other's lives. I know you're proud and stubborn, but it's not worth the price, believe me.'

'But, Lisa, why did he treat me that way? Why did he humiliate me like that? I mean, when he came back from London....' Her voice trailed away, remembering that awful night, the words that haunted her.

'Jackie, I don't know that. But there must have been a reason. Ask him.'

'*Ask* him! How can you say that? How could I do that!'

Lisa sighed and shifted her position, curling her legs underneath her. 'Listen to me, Jackie. In four years of marriage I've learned one thing: understanding each other doesn't just happen. You have to make it happen. Keep talking, keep asking. Never assume anything.'

'But I'm not married to Matt!'

'But you love him. That's what counts.'

Jacqueline made no reply.

Behind the big glasses Lisa's eyes were serious, searching. 'Remember you told me Matt came up to you on the beach? He wanted to talk to you then, but you wouldn't let him. You ran away. Why? Can't you give the man a chance?'

Memory flashed through her mind—the feeling of his skin against hers. His kiss. The terrifying thought that she might give in to him and show him the power he still held over her.

'I couldn't. I just couldn't!'

Lisa sighed, exasperated. 'You're two of a kind. You won't give each other half a chance. But somebody has got to break that vicious circle. Now it's your turn.'

'My turn? What do you mean?'

'I mean, if you want him, you'd better do something before it's too late. He's only human, too, Jackie. You wouldn't give him a chance. Now it's up to you. Go and talk to him. Say you're sorry—anything.'

'Oh, Lisa, I couldn't do that!'

'Jackie!' Lisa took her by the shoulders and shook her. 'Jackie! It's your pride, or him!'

Carefully and deliberately slowly she drove back to Osu,

past the petrol station, the bakery, the kiosk. On the street corners people stood or sat talking. Most of the vendors had gone home and the food stalls were all closed. It was late. Would Matt have gone to bed already? If she was going to talk to him, she'd have to do it tonight. By tomorrow her courage would have deserted her.

The light in the main living-room was off. Quietly she walked into the hall. There was a light on in Matt's room. Her legs were shaking and her hands were clammy. She brushed the hair away from her face, feeling the stickiness of her skin and the dampness of her hair.

I'm a mess, she thought. I need a drink. She went back to the kitchen, poured some of Matt's Scotch and took it back with her to the flat. I can't do it. I can't do it, she thought in desperation.

I'll make a pact, she thought suddenly. I'll take a shower, get myself presentable, and then if the light is still on I'll know it's a sign that things will be all right and I'll talk to him. If the light's out I'll know it's useless.

When she was a child she'd make deals like this a hundred times over, calling on fate to give her signs. For some reason it made her feel a little more confident. Or was it the whisky? Well, no matter. She undressed and got into the shower. The cool water on her warm skin refreshed her and made her feel better. She brushed her teeth, trying to erase all traces of whisky. She put on a skirt and blouse and combed her hair back into a pony tail. She grimaced at her reflection in the mirror. Nice little schoolgirl.

Don't stand there. Get going. Her courage almost deserted her then and there. She tiptoed through the living room into the hall and closed her eyes. Then slowly she opened them.

The light was still on.

Her heart pounded like a sledgehammer and fear rose to her throat. What am I going to say? she thought in rising panic.

Something will come to you.

She took a deep breath and knocked on the door, her legs trembling.

'Who is it?'

'It's me, Jackie.'

There was silence for an infinitesimal moment.

'All right. Come in.'

He was sitting at his desk in jeans and a white T-shirt, working. The air-conditioner was humming and the room felt cool. She closed the door behind her and leaned against it.

'Well, what can I do for you?' His face was smooth and expressionless.

'I wanted to apologise.'

'What for?' His voice was cool and distant.

'For what I said, for that stupid argument we had this evening.'

'Oh.' He waved his hand. 'Forget it.'

Her mouth was dry. 'I don't want to forget it.'

He shrugged. 'I don't know what you mean. Suit yourself.'

So he had his pride too. He wasn't giving an inch. If Lisa was right, she'd hurt him and now he had withdrawn behind that terrible, unapproachable mask. Help from him was not forthcoming. Despair overwhelmed her and she bit her lip.

'Matt, I'm sorry we're always fighting.'

'You'll be leaving soon and it'll be all over.' He didn't look at her, but his eyes were fixed on some point on his desk.

'I don't want to leave, Matt!' She felt as though she

were jumping off a cliff, down, down, down. She squeezed her eyes shut, opened them again.

Matt's face was a mask of indifference. 'That wasn't exactly the impression I had.'

It was as if she were gripped by a whirlwind, unable to resist its force. She struggled to keep her thoughts clear, but she couldn't think. She couldn't think! Lisa's words hammered through her brain. *'Someone's got to break that vicious circle. Now it's your turn!'* And then the words came flying out and she had no control over them.

'I don't want to fight you any more, Matt! It hurts too much. I was going away not because I hated you, but because ... because....' She bit her lip to stop it from trembling and she tasted salty tears. Somewhere in her rational mind she knew she was breaking down that carefully built up wall of her defences, but she couldn't stop herself now. 'I couldn't take it any more, Matt, thinking you were playing with me, treating me like some cheap little no-good....' She covered her face with her hands. Oh God, she thought, what am I doing? He'll laugh his heart out.

'You didn't believe me.' His voice was very low and she raised her head, surprised to hear the sudden change in his tone. He looked at her bleakly.

'You wouldn't talk to me and I didn't know how to get through to you, Jackie. It was all there was left to say, and you didn't believe me.'

She averted her gaze, not wanting to see the hurt in his eyes. 'No.'

'Why not?'

'I ... I wasn't expecting it. I thought you were....'

'Saying it to keep you on the job?'

'Yes.'

'Jackie, I don't play with love. I've had all the heartache I'll need for a lifetime.' There was bitterness in his voice and he looked at her with dark, sad eyes.

Diane. Always Diane.

'Did you love her very much?' She had to ask the question. She had to know.

The corners of his mouth pulled down. 'Diane? Did I love Diane? No, I don't believe love is the right word. Obsession maybe. Fascination, folly, insanity.... I confused it with the real thing, I know that now.' He raked his fingers through his hair. He looked tired and weary.

Jacqueline swallowed painfully. 'Matt, why were you so upset when she sent you that letter? Why weren't you glad to have it finished and over with?' Her voice was soft and barely audible. Vaguely she wondered if she had any right to ask these questions.

'Oh, Jackie, try to understand. That whole affair was so absurd and so unreal. I'd never failed anything before, never really loused up something important, except this impossible relationship. My pride was hurt, shattered. I never in my life felt so totally humiliated. So I went out and got sloshed.'

'You weren't sloshed.'

He waved his hand. 'Well, whatever.'

Jacqueline said nothing.

'There is something I'd like to know,' Matt said after a while. 'That night I came back from London—why did you do that?'

'Why?' Her face grew hot with embarrassment. 'I didn't plan it, if that's what you mean. It just ... it just happened. I've never in my life....' Her voice trailed away and she dared not look at him.

'You scared the hell out of me.'

'I *scared* you? How? Why?' She stared at him, not comprehending.

'I was scared of my emotions, what I was feeling for

you. When you touched me ... well, you must have
noticed it didn't leave me exactly cold.'

Jacqueline looked away. 'Was that so terrible?'

'Oh, Jackie, don't you see? I didn't trust my feelings. I
didn't trust you. I was raw with hurt and anger. Diane
had dumped me and somehow I had to get myself together again. I didn't want to feel anything, experience
emotions I wasn't ready to deal with again. And then
there were you with nothing on but a flimsy nightgown,
playing games with me.'

'I wasn't playing games!'

He looked deep into her eyes and she felt herself go
limp under his stare.

'I'm sorry I misunderstood your intentions,' he said
slowly. 'I guess that makes us even now.' He walked over
to the window and stared into the darkness outside,
hands thrust into his jeans pockets.

Jacqueline felt deadly tired. Her legs were heavy and
she sat down on a carved stool, hands in her lap. This
conversation was getting them nowhere, it seemed. But
at least they were talking instead of fighting. Her eyes
were fixed on the broad expanse of his back and she
wondered what was going through his mind. Everything
was so complicated.

'You know, Jackie, when you came here, I didn't want
you—for both personal and business reasons. But I was
proved wrong on many counts.' He turned to face her.
'You are everything Diane was not. You have a heart and
a head.' He paused, looking at her darkly. 'You are good
at your work and I can count on you. I started appreciat-
ing you on a professional level, but I was attracted to
you too. But I didn't give my feelings much thought
until that time we were in Tamale. I was suddenly overwhelmed by the thought that I might be in love with
you and I backed off—fast. I wasn't ready for love. I

didn't want to get involved again so soon, and so I made some bad mistakes.' He sighed heavily. 'I don't know if any of this makes sense to you.'

'I think so.' It was clear to her now why he had behaved the way he had. Why he had withdrawn from her so suddenly when he'd kissed her in Tamale. Why he hadn't kissed her at all after he'd taken her to dinner on her birthday.

Matt was still standing near the window, looking at her broodingly. 'And then there was David.'

'*David?*'

'I could never figure out what went on between the two of you. I didn't think it was love; the pieces didn't fit.'

Jacqueline's throat thickened with helplessness. 'Oh, Matt! Why is everything so complicated? I didn't want it to be! David and I....'

'He told me about it the night of the beach party.'

'What did he say?'

'He said you were friends. Period. Because you wanted it that way.'

She nodded.

'Jackie, we haven't been able to understand each other very well, have we? And if you're staying, maybe we should start over and try again. Make it simple and uncomplicated.'

She swallowed at the constriction in her throat. 'Yes.'

'Come here, Jackie.' Matt held out his hands and she went to him in a blind daze and put her hands in his.

'Look at me.'

It was very silent as their eyes met, each searching for truth in the face of the other.

'I love you, Jackie.' He spoke the words slowly and deliberately.

'I love you, Matt.'

For one agonising moment nothing happened. Then his arms gathered her up against him and the wild warmth of love flooded her being. Her face was pressed against his chest and she was barely able to breathe.

'Oh God,' he groaned, his face in her hair. 'Why did we do this to each other?' Then in an almost violent gesture he lifted up her face and kissed her. There was no restraint in his kiss and she trembled in his arms, overwhelmed by the emotions sweeping through her. His hands slid under her shirt, stroking her bare back. There was nothing in her mind now but the sweet ecstasy of his touch—no words, no thoughts. All self-control left her, but it didn't matter now. It didn't matter. She kissed him back hungrily, losing herself in the waves of love washing over her.

He released her slowly, taking her face in his hands. 'I'm sorry,' he said hoarsely. 'I'm sorry I hurt you that night I came back from London. I didn't understand.'

'Matt, oh, Matt....' Her voice broke and tears welled up in her eyes. It was all too much.

'Don't cry, don't cry.' He held her tightly against his chest, stroking her hair.

'Oh Matt, you don't know how I feel!' There were no words for the relief she felt and the joy that filled her.

'I do, I do.' He lifted her face and smiled down into her eyes. 'Relief. Pure, unadulterated relief.' He took her hand and pulled her towards the bed. 'Kissing is easier lying down.' Gently he pushed her down, putting his face against her breast. She could feel his hunger and his need for her and she closed her eyes, moving her hands slowly down his back.

'Hold me, Jackie. Hold me.'

She had never experienced the feelings now rushing through her. The ecstasy was almost terrifying in its intensity, leaving her weak and trembling.

After a while Matt slowly raised his head and his eyes looked darkly into hers.

'I have to warn you,' he said in a low voice. 'You'd better marry me. You'd better not tell me you don't believe in marriage!'

Jacqueline laughed softly. 'I'm old-fashioned when it comes to marriage. I like the real thing—commitment, strings attached and everything.'

'Good. That's exactly what I wanted to hear.'

She pulled his face towards her, kissed him drunkenly. She felt his hands on her breasts, caressing her tenderly.

'You're warm and soft and beautiful,' he whispered.

'Matt, oh, Matt!' She had no more words, only the need for him to go on touching her, kissing her.

'I love you,' he said hoarsely. 'I love you so very much.'

Everything around them suddenly went dark. With an asthmatic gasp the air-conditioner shuddered to a stop. For a few minutes they lay silently in each other's arms, but the electricity didn't come back on.

'I'd better get some candles,' Jacqueline whispered in Matt's ear.

'No.' His arms tightened around her. 'Later, later.'

Harlequin Salutes...

Rachel Lindsay

CAGE OF GOLD
HOUSE OF LORRAINE
THE TAMING OF LAURA
PRINCE FOR SALE
SECRETARY WIFE
ALIEN CORN

Six best-selling Harlequin books
by a world-famous author.

Each volume, attractively bound in
a uniquely designed cover, is a warm
and moving love story—the sort of story
that only an author as sensitive and
imaginative as Rachel Lindsay can produce.

Look for these beautiful books in June
at your favorite store.

4 FREE

Harlequin Romances

TAKE THESE 4 Harlequin Romances FREE

as advertised on TV

Thrill to romantic, aristocratic Istanbul, and the tender love story of a girl who built a barrier around her emotions in ANNE HAMPSON's "Beyond the Sweet Waters" . . . a Caribbean island is the scene setting for love and conflict in ANNE MATHER's "The Arrogant Duke" . . . exciting, sun-drenched California is the locale for romance and deception in VIOLET WINSPEAR's "Cap Flamingo" . . . and an island near the coast of East Africa spells drama and romance for the heroine in NERINA HILLIARD's "Teachers Must Learn."

Harlequin Romances . . . 6 exciting novels published each month! Each month you will get to know interesting, appealing, true-to-life people . . . . You'll be swept to distant lands you've dreamed of visiting . . . . Intrigue, adventure, romance, and the destiny of many lives will thrill you through each Harlequin Romance novel.

Get all the latest books before they're sold out!

As a Harlequin subscriber you actually receive your personal copies of the latest Romances immediately after they come off the press, so you're sure of getting all 6 each month.

Cancel your subscription whenever you wish!

You don't have to buy any minimum number of books. Whenever you decide to stop your subscription just let us know and we'll cancel all further shipments.

Your FREE gift includes

- *Anne Hampson* — Beyond the Sweet Waters
- *Anne Mather* — The Arrogant Duke
- *Violet Winspear* — Cap Flamingo
- *Nerina Hilliard* — Teachers Must Learn

FREE GIFT CERTIFICATE

and Subscription Reservation

Mail this coupon today!

In U.S.A.:	In Canada:
Harlequin Reader Service	Harlequin Reader Service
MPO Box 707	649 Ontario Street
Niagara Falls, NY 14302	Stratford, Ontario
	N5A 6W4

Harlequin Reader Service:

Please send me my 4 Harlequin Romance novels
FREE Also, reserve a subscription to the 6 NEW
Harlequin Romance novels published each month
Each month I will receive 6 NEW Romance novels at
the low price of $1.25 each (Total — $7.50 a month)
There are no shipping and handling or any other
hidden charges I may cancel this arrangement at any
time, but even if I do, these first 4 books are still mine
to keep

_____

NAME   (PLEASE PRINT)

_____

ADDRESS

_____

CITY   STATE/PROV   ZIP/POSTAL CODE

Offer not valid to present subscribers

Offer expires December 31, 1980   0055642

Prices subject to change without notice.